D1524998

Pumpkin Spice
&
Deadly Heist

The Nosy Paralegal Mystery Series

Book One

Tanya R. Taylor

WITHDRAWN FROM
RAPIDES PARISH LIBRARY

RAPIDES PARISH LIBRARY
Alexandria, Louisiana JN

Copyright© 2022 Tanya R. Taylor
All Rights Reserved.

No portion of this work may be reproduced, copied or transmitted in any form without the written consent of the Author.

This is a fictitious work in its entirety. The author bears no responsibility for any possible similarities concerning names, places or events.

ABOUT THE AUTHOR

 Tanya R. Taylor is a Readers' Favorite Award Winning Author. She has been writing ever since she was a child and published her first book titled: *A Killing Rage* as a young adult. She is now the author of both fiction and non-fiction literature. Her books have made Amazon Kindle's Top 100 Paid Best-sellers' List in several categories. Tanya writes in various genres including: Paranormal Romance, Fantasy, Thrillers, Science fiction, Mystery and Suspense.

Her book *Cornelius*, the first installment in a successful series, climbed to number one in Amazon's Teen & Young-adult Multi-generational Family Fiction category. And *INFESTATION: A Small Town Nightmare* and *CARA* are both number one international bestsellers.

1

Forty-eight-year-old Barbara Sandosa walked into the law firm of J. Wilfred & Co. at ten past nine on Monday morning, carrying a large, brown paper bag with both hands. She was wearing her favorite short-sleeved, yellow cotton blouse and a matching yellow and white striped skirt that stopped just above the knees. The yellow chrysanthemum tucked in her shoulder-length auburn hair, just behind her right ear, gave her the carefree look she was after.

"Good morning! Good morning!" she sang right past the thirty-year-old receptionist, Mary Grisham, who wore thick eyeglasses and no makeup.

"Good morning, Barbara," Mary replied, unenthusiastically.

Entering the open room adjacent to the reception area, Barbara rested the bag on her desk and proceeded to sit down.

"What's in the bag, Barb?" Young Harry Buford leaned in from his chair and went to have a look.

"Naughty boy!" Barbara spanked his hand. "You know I like to unveil the goodies myself."

Harry was fifteen years Barbara's junior. He was a five-foot ten inches tall, rotund redhead with freckles and was a spiffy dresser. Hired two years earlier as Barbara's assistant since the law firm only had one paralegal at the time, more than once a client had mistaken him for a junior lawyer.

"It smells heavenly!" he said, sniffing deeply.

Barbara opened the bag and pulled out the cupcakes. "They're pumpkin spice. I baked them early this morning so that they'll be nice and fresh. Want one?"

"Do I?" Harry quickly snatched one and wasted no time biting into it. "Hmmm….hmmmm…good." He felt the icing escaping through the corner of his mouth, but couldn't care less as he kept biting in.

"Glad you like it. I'm gonna take one to *frown face* over there. Hopefully, this will be the miracle that forces her to crack a smile. But then again, considering it's been ages since her skin cells have been moistened with a smile, her face might crack altogether and we'll have Frankenstein working with us. Isn't that frightening?"

Harry chuckled as he was about to finish his cupcake. "It's worth a try," he said. "May I have another?"

"Sure, go ahead."

She picked up one using a napkin she'd dropped in the bag and started around the desk. "The limit for you is two, Harry. Mr. Wilfred would kill me if he knew I had pastries and didn't offer him any.

"Gotcha." He happily bit down into another cupcake.

The law offices of J. Wilfred & Co. were situated in a small office building near Sandpiper Lake in Grenhurst. A young, dynamic attorney thirty years earlier, Jack Wilfred had paid cash for the land priced well below the market value to a retired war veteran who desperately needed the sale to go through in order to fund his wife's operation. Feeling sorry for the guy who was practically giving away his property for pennies on the dollar, Wilfred gave him an extra ten thousand, outside of the sales agreement. Though highly successful at the time, he was often mindful *to keep his feet on the ground and his nose out of the air* like his mother had preached to him during those years he was in law school.

"I want my son to always have a humble heart," she used to tell him. *"I hate snooty lawyers! Money and status should never change a person who wipes their behind like everyone else does. The nerve of them to suddenly think they're better than other people!"* Sally-Joe Wilfred never minced her words even well into old age and her only son, Jack, loved her for it.

Four years after sealing the property deal, Wilfred had turned the beach house he had built on the property into his new law firm, and the view was spectacular. He renovated the place to make it look like an office and added more windows so that clients could see the glistening lake just outside and surrounding greenery while they waited.

The place consisted of a small reception area, some waiting chairs and a larger open area of approximately three hundred square feet where Barbara's and Harry's desks were. Just off a small corridor on the right were two attorney's offices, but only one was currently occupied—by Jack Wilfred himself. The restroom was on the eastern end while the kitchen was located on the western end closest to Wilfred's office, which also happened to be the second largest room in the building.

"Is Barbara here yet?" Wilfred asked Mary via the intercom in his usual gruff voice.

"She just walked in and is standing right in front of me," Mary replied, quite eagerly.

"Ask her to get in here."

"I'm sure you heard him," Mary told Barbara with a mischievous grin on her face. "And thanks for the cupcake."

Barbara pitied her for being the miserable wretch she thought she was. "You're very welcome," she replied. "Don't choke on it, now."

"I'll try not to."

As Barbara walked away, Mary dumped the cupcake into her nearby trash bin.

Barbara made a quick stop at her desk and picked up a couple of cupcakes for her boss.

"Where are you going?" Harry asked.

"Mr. Wilfred wants to see me," she said. "Sounded...well...like himself."

"Oh boy." Harry slowly shook his head.

"Wish me luck."

"You got it."

Wilfred's mahogany desk and tufted leather chair stood directly facing the doorway, Behind them, the sun shone briskly through the window blinds, brightening the entire room.

Wilfred loved the feel of the sun's rays on his back as he sat there and worked; made him feel more alive. Sometimes it was the only thing that elevated his mood since he'd been a widower for fourteen years and hadn't been quite the same since his wife, Leslia, died.

He was sitting at his desk when Barbara walked in.

"Good morning, sir. You wanted to see me?" she asked, cheerfully.

"Morning to you. As a matter of fact, I do," he replied.

"Just so you know, Mary lied to you, sir. I didn't *just* walk in the door, like she said. I was here for a few minutes already."

"I'm not concerned about that, Barbara. You're always a little late and I've gotten used to it over all these years." Then he looked down. "What's with the slippers?"

Barbara's eyes followed his gaze. "Oh! I hadn't realized I'd thrown on the wrong shoes rushing out the door this morning. I'll go back and get my work shoes."

"Nah! Don't worry about it. You rarely ever leave the office anyway, other than for lunch. If they're comfortable, wear them, but don't show up in them tomorrow."

"Yes, sir." She walked over to him. "I brought you some cupcakes."

"What kind?" he asked.

"Pumpkin spice."

"Pumpkin spice?" His face softened a bit. "Leslia used to make pumpkin spice cookies for the kids when they were growing up. They absolutely loved them. When she got older, she couldn't handle all of that baking anymore." He paused for a moment, then managed a smile. "You think the kids miss her pastries? I miss them even more."

"I know what you mean, sir." She handed them to him. "I hope you enjoy these. I baked them early this morning."

"Don't you ever sleep, Barbara?" He rested them in front of him.

"I only need about five or six hours shuteye these days. Living alone—no husband, no kids—you have to keep yourself occupied, you know?"

He nodded.

"I go to bed at ten and usually wake up around three or four o'clock every morning. Don't even need coffee some days," she went on.

"Well, that's what I called you in here for. Can you make me a cup of cappuccino there in the kitchen? Mary's coffee tastes like poop!"

Barbara laughed. "Certainly, sir! But I'll have you know...I'm not about to take on her job, so she'd better learn to get it right."

"Give her a few tips," he suggested. "And really—getting me coffee isn't in anyone's job description. I'm just sometimes too tired or lazy to make it myself."

"No worries, sir. I'll get your coffee anytime you want—just like before you hired *Miss pain in the butt* out there."

"Leave her be, Barbara! The woman has a right to be grumpy. She lost her mother two months ago and they were very close."

"You hired her three years ago, sir. What's the excuse for the other thirty-four months?"

Grinning, Wilfred shook his head. "As long as I don't get any serious complaints from my clients, she can stay as long as she wants."

"By all means. Just allow her to make the lives of your other employees miserable."

He grimaced. "Harry doesn't seem to have a problem with her. Does he?"

"Harry barely notices her, so I doubt he'd be bothered either way. Don't get me wrong—I wouldn't want anyone to lose their job. I was just hoping you can put her in the basement or somewhere so I wouldn't have to see her every second."

Wilfred laughed heartily. "You are something else!"

"One cappuccino coming up, sir!" she said, leaving the room.

---

2

*A*t 10:22 A.M., a tall, husky man walked into the law firm of J. Wilfred & Co. He was wearing loose-fitting denim jeans and a blue tee shirt, and looking rather nervous.

"May I help you, sir?" Mary asked, the moment he walked through the door.

With his hands shoved into his jeans pocket, he approached the reception desk. "Yeah, I need to see Mr. Wilfred."

"Do you have an appointment?"

"I need an appointment?" He seemed confused.

"Yes. That's how we operate around here," she said.

Mary was not very pleasant with those clients or potential clients she suspected weren't people of means, per se. She figured the regular folk were troublemakers anyway and felt she could always convince Wilfred that another lowlife was disrupting her day and the quietude of the firm.

"Well, I need to see him now because it's urgent. I don't have time to make any appointment," the man said.

She looked rather demeaningly at him behind those lightly tinted eyeglasses of hers. "It seems we had a slight dip in communication here. I just told you that you need an appointment to see Mr. Wilfred. Just because you gave me some story about urgency doesn't mean it changes the rules."

He leaned against the counter, glaring down at her. "Do I look like I'm asking you, miss? I told you..." his voice quickly escalating to a shout, "…that I need to see Mr. Wilfred. I don't care if I have to wait here all day, I need to see him."

Mary abruptly stood up. "You couldn't have just spewed all of that spit in my face telling me what you want. I said you will need an appointment and if you would like for me to make one for you, I will gladly do so the minute you step away from my desk!"

"Look, lady…"

Just then, Barbara hurried out there as Harry looked on from his desk, relishing the entertainment. He'd seen Mary in action numerous times being sassy with the clients and he wondered why she was allowed to get away with it. Oftentimes, Mr. Wilfred hadn't even heard a word of it.

"Sir, what is it?" Barbara asked the man as Mary stood there looking at her as if she'd overstepped her boundaries.

"I was just telling this *person* in a dress that I need to see Mr. Wilfred urgently," he replied. "If he's busy, I'll wait; but she doesn't seem to understand that!"

"*Person*, huh?" Mary scoffed. "At least I'm a part of the human race. Can't say the same for you by the way you've been acting—which is *ghet-to*.

"She didn't just say that," Harry muttered, shaking his head.

The man looked at Mary as if he wished to choke the very life out of her, then he turned to Barbara again. "Wait a minute…" he started. "This *is* a law firm, right?"

"Yes, it is," Barbara quickly nodded.

"I wondered for a minute there if I wasn't in the jungle."

"Believe me, you're not." She gave Mary a reprimanding glance and the receptionist soon sat down. It wasn't purely out of respect for

Barbara either, considering she was more senior to her; Mary simply concluded the situation was going sideways and she no longer cared.

Barbara gently pulled the man aside. "My name is Barbara. I'm Mr. Wilfred's assistant. May I ask your name and what's the nature of the urgency?"

He hesitated for a moment, then said, "I guess it's not private anyway. My name is Alan Danzabar and the other day I was named as an accomplice in a bank robbery that resulted in the shooting death of the security guard. The guys involved said I was right there with them and even that I was the mastermind behind the whole thing, but I had nothing to do with it. I was even taken into the police station and interrogated for hours on end. Surprisingly, they didn't throw me in the slammer, but I'm pretty sure they're coming back to do the deed. I can feel it in my bones and I need to see Mr. Wilfred before that happens."

"I know the case you're referring to," Barbara replied. "You have a seat right there," she gestured toward the seating area. "And I'll have a word with Mr. Wilfred."

"Thanks." He took a seat, glancing annoyingly at Mary while Barbara headed to the back.

As Mary started unwrapping a cherry lollipop, she stared Alan down as if he was filthy, twisted gum beneath her shoe.

Harry Buford, in the meanwhile, pretended to get back to work. The fact was, he couldn't wait to see how the drama would unfold—if Wilfred would entertain the guy much to Mary's dissatisfaction or if he'd turn him down cold.

Barbara returned, moments later, and Alan quickly stood up.

"Mr. Wilfred has an appointment in a half hour, but he's agreed to see you for a few minutes. Afterwards, if necessary, we'll set up another appointment for you when it's convenient for you both," she said to Alan.

"Sounds good to me."

"Right this way," Barbara said.

* * * *

"Were you responsible for all of that raucous out there?" Wilfred asked at his desk after Alan and Barbara walked in.

"I'm partly to blame, sir," Alan responded. "Your receptionist is responsible for about ninety-nine percent of it. Nonetheless, I apologize."

"All right, have a seat. But just so you know for next time, you can't come in here and demand service as if we're entitled to drop everything just for you. We have a structure in place and you need to respect that."

Alan nodded it away, opting not to spend the little time he was afforded with the attorney defending himself against the receptionist. He figured he might have lost that battle anyway.

Barbara took a seat in the other chair a few feet away from Alan's. After crossing her legs, she rested the white legal pad atop her lap and held the ball point pen ready.

"Are you ready to begin, Barbara?" Wilfred asked.

"Yes, sir," she quickly replied.

"So, what can we do for you today?" Wilfred looked at Alan.

The man shifted slightly in his chair and explained to him what he'd already told Barbara.

"So, why would anyone say you took part in a crime if it wasn't true?" Wilfred asked.

"I have no idea. Maybe it's a case of mistaken identity," Alan said.

"Mistaken identity, huh?" Wilfred puckered his lips. "Did you grow up in Grenhurst?"

"Yeah, I did."

"This is a small town. How many people out there do you think look exactly like you?"

The question seemed to catch Alan off guard.

"You go on and think about that," Wilfred continued. "By the way… are you a twin?"

"No." Alan shook his head.

"Well, how do you suppose that three people pointed you out as being a conspirator to a crime?"

A few moments of silence ensued.

Barbara was recording in shorthand and feeling a bit awkward for Alan. What the young man obviously didn't know was that J. Wilfred usually asked his potential clients the hard questions—even offended some by putting them on the proverbial stand and drilling them before they ever got to the real one. And not as their attorney, but as the prosecutor. This behavior caught Barbara by surprise when she first started working for Wilfred in the early days. His style of questioning hadn't struck her as effective for getting new clients. However, she soon realized that it was what had helped build his reputation as one of the best attorneys in town.

"I've wondered about that and just can't understand how they can say I was there with them in that bank, masked and everything, and even planned it when I was nowhere near the bank that day," Alan finally said.

"Do you know these guys?" Wilfred leaned forward.

"I went to middle school with one of them—Dean Paltrow. The others I've only seen with him a couple of times at the bar I frequent.

Wilfred got the name of the bar and Barbara made note of it.

"How was your relationship with Dean?" Wilfred asked.

"I wouldn't call him a friend. Sure, we made small talk a couple of times, but we never hung out together or anything like that. I didn't really dig the crowd he was running with even when we were in middle school. Everybody knows Dean's had kind of a rough upbringing with his mom missing in action when he was a kid and his alcoholic dad having to raise him. So, he turned out to be a bully, you know. I guess kind of striking back for how his dad treated him with all those whippings and stuff."

"The bullied became the bully," Wilfred sat back again.

Alan nodded. "Pretty much."

"Did he ever bully you?"

"Never. I guess because he could see I was no push over. I didn't have an easy time myself growing up and I learned pretty quick how to defend myself. That was no secret while we were in school."

"I see."

"Rick Santos and Ben Johnson were Dean's right-hand guys, I guess you can say. I don't know anything much about them at all."

Wilfred studied him for a few moments, then took a sip of his cappuccino.

"That must be cold by now," Barbara said. "Would you like for me to make you another cup, sir?"

"No...no..." he replied. "It's almost gone anyway."

"Yes, sir."

She looked at Alan, who was now rubbing his hands together. "Are you all right, Mr. Danzabar?"

He suddenly burst into tears. "I can't go to jail for a crime I didn't commit! I'm twenty-eight-years-old and have never even gotten as much as a parking ticket. There's no way I would disappoint my parents, who taught me about values and morals, to go out there and rob a bank with a bunch of lowlifes and on top of that kill a man—all for money. I have a two-year-old daughter who needs me to be there for her." He turned to Wilfred. "I'm innocent Mr. Wilfred. I need you to believe that! These guys are trying to set me up to take the fall and I have no idea why because I've never done anything to any of them. Please help me."

Wilfred sighed, looking away for a while. Then he stood up and peered outside the window at the lake.

Everyone knew Jack Wilfred didn't take on every case that managed to find its way through his front door. He was selective to the point that more than fifty percent of matters, he abruptly turned down. Not because he felt he couldn't effectively defend those involved, but because he doubted their honesty. One thing Jack Wilfred couldn't stand was a liar. Being guilty, in his books, didn't equate to being deceitful.

"If you did it, I'm giving you this one last chance to tell me the truth," he said to Alan with his back still turned.

Alan had now dried his tears. "I swear, I'm not guilty. I had nothing to do with any of it!" he exclaimed.

Wilfred turned around and sat down again, then looked him dead in the eye. "All right. I agree to represent you, but I'll let you know in no uncertain terms that if I find out at any point that you lied to me, I'll drop you quicker than a sack of potatoes and leave you on your natural own. You hear me?"

"I hear you, sir." Alan quickly asserted.

"So, you have between right now and the time before you walk out of that door to tell me if there's anything you weren't truthful about. If you're guilty, it doesn't mean I won't take on the case once you've leveled with me about everything. I won't go in court and lie for you, but I'll give you the best representation money can buy. I tell you that."

"I've told you the truth, sir," Alan replied, softly.

"How are you set financially?"

"I work as a mechanic for a friend's shop. The job doesn't pay very well, but I'm a good saver, so I have a few thousand in the bank. Since I live on my parents' property in an old cottage out back, I don't have to pay any rent. So that's why I'm able to save a little something out of every paycheck."

"Do you have about fifty thousand tucked away on that account?" Wilfred asked.

"Fifty thousand?" Alan was clearly shocked.

"I…I…don't have that much. Is that how much it would cost to retain you?"

"I'm afraid so—for some other people," Wilfred said. "But if you can come up with a measly one thousand dollars, I'll help you out."

"Just… a thousand?" Alan's face lit up.

Barbara was smiling. She'd seen that scenario before.

"Yep. That's it," Wilfred replied.

"So, how much would I have for you when the case is over?"

"Nothing. Unless you want to buy me a cup of coffee."

Alan glanced at Barbara, then turned to Wilfred again. "I wasn't...expecting that. I figured what I had saved wouldn't have been enough, but I would've tried my best to raise the rest somehow."

"Whatever you have left, save it for your daughter," Wilfred told him. "Kids are expensive."

"Why—thank you, sir! Thank you so much!"

The seasoned attorney took a card out of his desk drawer and handed it to Alan. "My cell number's on there if you need to reach me. Right now, it's obvious that the police haven't arrested you because they have nothing to hold you with. But if the detectives working the case believe you were involved, I can guarantee they're trying to find something. If things go from bad to worse, just give me a call. In the meantime,

Barbara here will have you fill out a form and she'll accept the retainer."

"Thanks so much, Mr. Wilfred." Alan got up, following Barbara's lead. "It's been a pleasure meeting you in person. I just wish it would've been under better circumstances."

"Pleasure meeting you too," Wilfred replied.

"Right this way." Barbara led the way to the door.

Alan followed her out of the office and into the main area.

"This will take just a few minutes," she said, heading over to her desk. "Please have a seat."

"Good morning," Harry said to him.

"Hi." Alan sat down in the black leather chair in front.

Barbara retrieved a form and a pen from her desk and gave them to him.

"Just fill in all of the information there and don't forget to insert your phone numbers and exact address."

"Sure." He glanced over it, then started filling it out.

"How will you be paying—by cash or check?" she asked.

"Do you take debit cards?"

"Yes, we do! Sorry for leaving that option out."

"No problem." He slid the card from his wallet and reached over the desk. "Here you go."

"Thanks." She was peering at her computer screen. "Come on! Come on!" She snarled, then looked his way again. "The system's moving pretty slow this morning. Guess it hasn't had its morning coffee yet!"

He managed a laugh and Harry did too.

"Mine's been this way for about a year now," Harry said. "Guess the coffee it's been getting is too darn weak. Probably needs to cut out the milk."

They all had a hearty laugh and as Barbara noticed how much lighter the atmosphere seemingly was for Alan, she felt good inside.

Just then, the door opened and Isaac Chamberlain, sixty-year-old millionaire and owner of the largest commercial shopping plaza in town walked in. Jack Wilfred had been his lawyer ever since he'd built his first plaza and opened the baby clothing store for his wife, Julia, some thirteen years ago.

"Good morning, Mr. Chamberlain!" Mary said, excitedly.

"Good morning, Mary. How's it going?" He smiled. "Is Jack in today?"

"Yes, sir. He's in his office. I'll let him know you're here. May I offer you a cup of coffee?"

"No, thanks. Just had one on the way here."

She picked up the handset. "Mr. Chamberlain's here to see you, sir."

"Send him on in," Wilfred replied.

She turned to Isaac. "He says you can go in now."

"Great!" He headed for the back, approaching Barbara and company on the way.

"Barbara, it's good to see you!" he said, as if she was the only one in the room.

"Hey there, Mr. Chamberlain. How's the madam?" she asked.

"Just fine. Just fine."

"Give her my regards."

"I surely will," he replied.

Pondering how the receptionist was more than willing to bend over backwards for that guy and how rude she'd been to him, Alan quietly handed Barbara the form.

Thanks," she said. "It can't be easy what you're going through, Mr. Danzabar. A man died, for goodness' sake! Being implicated in a bank robbery is bad enough, but when you get murder in the mix there…"

"It's pretty bad, all right," he agreed. "I've barely slept since the whole thing came up and my work at the shop is suffering. Good thing the boss and I are good friends or he might not be as patient."

"That sucks," Harry chimed in. "I know what it's like to be accused of something I was totally innocent of. One time, when I was a kid…"

"Harry, let's not keep Mr. Danzabar here any longer than necessary," Barbara interrupted. I'm sure he has to get to work or something."

"Yeah. Sorry about that," Harry replied, quietly. "I tend to run off the rail sometimes."

"Your card." She handed Alan his debit card.

"Thanks for everything," he said, getting up. "Mr. Wilfred is a good guy—one of a kind."

"He's the best!" Barbara proudly asserted. "Now, make sure you keep his card handy and call if there are any further developments."

"I will," he said.

She got up as well. "Allow me to see you out."

They headed to the front area again and Alan glanced at Mary.

"Have a nice day now," she said as he was leaving.

He didn't bother to respond.

Barbara walked over to Mary's desk. "You could have easily called me if you were having an issue out here with a potential client."

"I know how to do my job," she replied matter-of-factly. I had the whole thing under control."

"Barely," Harry chimed in from his desk.

"Mr. Harry Buford—no one's talking to you!" she blurted.

"Well, next time, before it becomes a shouting match, do your job and call me if I'm not in the immediate area," Barbara told her without a blink. "I'm still in charge of running this office."

"I'm aware of your position here, Barbara. Believe me."

For a second, Barbara wondered what she meant by the way she stated it, but didn't bother to ask.

"That's good to know." She scanned the desk. "Enjoyed the cupcake?"

"Every last crumb," Mary answered with a straight face.

Barbara returned to her desk, giving Harry a wink as she sat down.

"Good job!" he whispered. "It's about time you reminded that prune who's second in command around here. You would've thought *she* was."

"I know. The guy already had some heavy stuff on his mind. He didn't need that drama," she replied.

"Exactly!"

3

Barbara kicked off her slippers after opening the front door of her cozy two-bedroom abode situated in the suburb of Wintry Shores. She'd left the office shortly after five o'clock and was looking forward to curling up on the couch with her latest mystery novel. But first, she planned on having a warm bubble bath and the leftovers of curried pork chops and rice from last evening.

She had Jack Wilfred to thank for her move into Wintry Shores from that one-bedroom apartment she hated in the noisy southern part of town. After six months of working for Wilfred, he made a call to the developer of the subdivision, asking him to reserve one of his two remaining lots for her. She'd made a great impression on him and also on his late wife, Leslia, especially with all the pastries Barbara had made and shared with them. He always said his Leslia knew a good baker when she saw one.

A month later, Barbara had a deed to the property right there on the cul-de-sac and four months after that her contractor had finished building her house. She painted it yellow that first year, then put a new coat of yellow paint on it every couple of years thereafter. The interior walls were all yellow too, except for the kitchen which she kept plain white, primarily since having a white kitchen reminded her of her mother's and all the time she spent watching her cook when she was a little girl.

Barbara headed straight to the bathroom and ran her bath water, then retrieved the lavender-scented candles from her bedroom. Although she felt for a bubble bath, she picked up the small package of Epsom Salt instead.

Working with Mary was no picnic and the mere thought of the woman made those muscles and nerves of hers scream for magnesium.

Soaking in the tub and feeling satiated by its warmth, her mind soon drifted on Alan Danzabar and how she had treated him.

"Idiot!" she muttered. "The day Mr. Wilfred fires her or she picks up and moves on will be the best day of my life."

After a few minutes replaying the scattered events of the day, she tilted her head back and tried to relax. Yet, Alan's case kept resurfacing.

What could possibly be the motive for someone to tell such a terrible lie about someone they barely knew? She wondered.

Sighing heavily, she said, "This is supposed to be relaxing time. Why don't I ever leave *work* at work?"

Minutes later, she got up and wrapped herself in her favorite white bathrobe when she heard the doorbell ring.

"Who is it?" she yelled, stepping into the hallway.

"It's Janet," went the shaky, little voice outside her front door.

Barbara sucked her teeth and headed to the door.

"Hi, Janet." She tried to conceal her annoyance from her seventy-five-year-old neighbor.

"Hi There! I saw your car on the driveway and figured you must be home by now," Janet stated, cheerfully.

Janet Shelby lived next door with her husband, Ralph, and their cat Ralph Jr., otherwise known as Ralphy. Their cat was named after Ralph due to the fact that the couple had no children. Barbara had once asked Janet since that was the case why the cat wasn't named after her instead, but Janet thought the whole idea was ridiculous anyway, but respected her husband's wishes.

"Just got home a while ago and was about to have dinner," Barbara told her.

"Oh! Do you have a minute? I promise I won't keep you long."

"Sure. Come on in." She stepped aside and Janet made her way over to the couch.

"Do you mind if I threw on something quickly?" Barbara asked.

"'Course not! Go right ahead."

On her way to the bedroom, Barbara couldn't fathom what Janet wanted to have a quick word about. Usually, her visits consisted of tea, cookies and conversation about the good old days. Barbara found the good old days quite interesting to hear about and she actually enjoyed

Janet's company too when *me time* wasn't calling her.

Janet was tall, thin and had the whitest hair Barbara had ever seen and a mouth that rarely stopped moving. She often wondered how old Ralph managed over there with her especially since they both were retired and had to look at each other a whole lot more these days. Whatever the reason for Janet's visit that day, Barbara hoped she wasn't the bearer of bad news.

"I hope I haven't kept you waiting too long." Barbara sat down after having thrown on a short-sleeved, light-blue blouse and a pair of blue shorts.

"Not at all," Janet replied. "I don't want to keep you, so I will get straight to the point." She started fiddling with her fingers which was a clear indication to Barbara that something *touchy* or important was coming next.

"We've been neighbors for a good long time, haven't we?" Janet said.

"Uh—huh.," Barbara's curiosity was now piquing.

"So, I...*we* were wondering—Ralph and I—since we're getting up in age and our days are pretty much numbered—also the fact that we don't have any children—if you would be so kind to take Ralphy in if something were to happen to us."

The request caught Barbara by surprise. "Ah...sure," she replied. "Sure, I'll take him in."

Janet smiled as a few moments of awkward silence sailed by.

"Well, that's great to know. I'll be sure to put that in writing for whenever the time comes so the process would be seamless," she said.

"Ralphy's a good boy and doesn't cause any trouble."

"I know. He's great," Barbara replied.

Something about that conversation didn't feel right to her. The request in and of itself wasn't so odd, but there was something different about Janet's demeanor that she couldn't quite put her finger on.

"Is everything all right with you and Ralph?" she asked.

"Oh yes! Everything's wonderful. Ralph is in great spirits in spite of his heart condition and dementia, and I'm doing just fine. Thanks for asking."

"Okay."

Janet stood up. "Don't want to keep you from your dinner any longer. Thanks so much, Barbara, for being here for all of us. You're a wonderful neighbor."

"Don't mention it."

As Barbara stood up, Janet went over and gave her the warmest hug, then headed for the door.

"Tea on Saturday?" Barbara thought to ask.

Janet stopped and looked back for a second. "We'll see."

Then she left.

Barbara closed the door behind her. "That was weird," she muttered. "Even for Janet."

She proceeded to the refrigerator for the leftovers and turned on the kitchen radio as she warmed up the food.

* * * *

The next morning...

Before heading to her car, Barbara bent over and picked up the newspaper. As usual, she intended to read it at the office.

Humming to the beat of a golden oldie, she'd had her morning coffee and was in a splendid mood, especially since the workload at the office promised to be minimal. Barbara enjoyed her job as a paralegal, but in recent years Wilfred rarely ever stepped inside of a courtroom. The office handled a lot of corporate matters and just a handful of civil and criminal cases each year. And ninety-nine percent of the cases that Wilfred ever defended in court, he won. Barbara particularly enjoyed accompanying him to court, intrigued by the matters at hand and the persuasive manner in which Wilfred put his point across to sway the judge and jury. The man was gifted, she thought, and his bank account always told the story.

At 8:55, she arrived at the office and hailed Mary as she walked by. She could feel her stare piercing her back, but didn't care. She was determined to have a great day and to keep a positive attitude.

"Good morning, Harry!" she sang, resting her purse next to her desk.

"Good morning to you!" he sang back.

"What's that?" She was looking at his drink.

"Lemongrass tea."

"What?"

"Lemongrass tea. They say it's good for keeping blood pressure in check."

"You're concerned about blood pressure at your age?" she asked. "You're only twenty-three."

"Yeah—and overweight and hypertensive, according to my doctor. Pre-hypertensive, actually," he clarified. "Even children are getting high blood pressure these days. Must be something in the water."

Barbara laughed. "In the water, huh? I didn't know you were pre-hypertensive. You never told me that."

"You never asked."

Barbara rolled her eyes. "Well, keep drinking the lemongrass if it works."

"Yep. That's the plan."

"Is the boss in yet?"

"Need you ask? He practically lives here."

"Tell me about it."

She headed toward the back and abruptly stopped at the kitchen.

"Good morning, Sir! How are we doing today?" She met Wilfred fiddling with the coffee maker.

"We're not doing so good. I can't get this bloody thing to work!" he barked.

"Let me take care of it."

He stepped aside and allowed her to do her thing.

"It's all good now," she said after getting it started and having placed his mug beneath the faucet. "Why on earth didn't you ask Mary to make this?"

"Because it's not her job. And besides, she never seems to get it right. I'd rather drink muddy water."

"Oh! That's harsh, Mr. Wilfred." Barbara chuckled.

"What's harsh is that poison she makes for me disguised as coffee—that's what's harsh!"

They both laughed it off, but Wilfred was as serious as a heart attack. Barbara was pleased to see that Mary hadn't been doing such a perfect job kissing up to their boss. Yet oddly, she still seemed to be getting her way most of the time.

She gave him the mug with the hot coffee after it was done. "There, you go."

"Thank you, Barbara."

He started to leave.

"By the way, have you finished the title deed for Rose Klonaris?"

"Yes. She's all set. Sent the docs to the bank yesterday."

"Perfect! I'm gonna get this coffee down, then I'll be off."

"Where to, sir? I don't recall you having an offsite appointment today," Barbara replied.

"I'm off to L.A. to see my daughter, Chelsea and the grandkids. I'm not a fan of her husband, John, but he'll stick around for now."

"That's nice, but on a weekday, sir? You usually reserve personal travels for weekends."

"Last I checked your name wasn't Leslia Jane Wilfred. I'm sixty years old and I think I should be able to pick up and go whenever the breeze hits me and I'm gonna do just that, little lady. This firm isn't running away and neither are you since you're in charge of it, remember? If anything comes up, let them know I'll be back day after tomorrow."

"Yes, sir," Barbara replied.

Wilfred left the office with a carry-on luggage bag and his briefcase twenty minutes later. Barbara ensured that he hadn't forgotten his passport like he did the last time.

Sometimes she worried about him being all alone in that great, big mansion he'd built for his beloved Leslia, with none of the kids around to keep him company. So, she felt somewhat responsible for him and out of gratitude for all he'd done for her, she took that responsibility very seriously.

After pouring herself a second cup of coffee, she sat at her desk and opened the newspaper.

"My goodness!" She almost burned her tongue upon taking a sip.

"What is it?" Harry asked.

"That Dean guy who was involved in the bank robbery the other day apparently confessed to a reporter that he has evidence that our client was a participant in the heist."

"Why would that detail be in the newspaper?" Harry asked.

Barbara thought for a few moments. "It's odd. I wonder what kind of evidence this guy has, though," she replied, contemplatively.

"Oh, no." Harry shook his head. "I sense we're in protective mode again. Don't forget your last stunt almost got us fired."

"Mr. Wilfred knew we had his best interest at heart, Harry! If we didn't break into that place, the police wouldn't have known where to find the evidence."

She was referring to a client the firm had taken on last year by the name of Katrina Willows. Katrina was adamant that a homeless man was responsible for her husband's murder when, in actuality, the murder weapon was tucked away in an old warehouse they owned— near the bridge under which the homeless man slept. Thanks to some private, although amateurish investigating, Barbara and Harry retrieved some vital information from a friend of the homeless guy who'd seen Mrs. Willows sneak inside of that warehouse late one night. Through some sneaking around of their own, they located the murder weapon and their unscrupulous client was duly arrested and charged.

"We were only protecting Mr. Wilfred from having that awful woman make a fool of him in the courtroom. And at the same time preventing an innocent man from being sent to the slammer for the rest of his life, or worse— executed. We did the right thing."

"Yeah—just probably the wrong way," Harry said.

"Well, I have no regrets," Barbara replied. "Do you?"

"None whatsoever."

"Great! Now that that's sorted out, we have to get to this Dean guy and find out what he knows."

Harry sighed. "You suspect our new client, Mr. Alan Danzabar, isn't being honest with Mr. Wilfred?"

"Not at all." She grimaced.

"So, why are we doing this?"

"To be on top of the game—just in case someone's really being played here." She picked up her purse. "Let's go."

"Now?"

"No better time."

"Okay… if you say so."

They both got up and made their way towards the door.

"We'll be out for a couple of hours," Barbara told Mary. "You can reach me on my cell if you need to."

"Sure thing, *Miss Paralegal slash Administrator.*"

Barbara shook her head, and she and Harry headed outside to her Toyota.

"That girl's a piece of work," Harry remarked, fastening his seatbelt.

"She needs an exorcism or something." Barbara put the gear in reverse and pulled off.

4

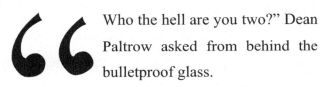Who the hell are you two?" Dean Paltrow asked from behind the bulletproof glass.

Barbara was speaking with him using the bolted phone on the prison wall and Harry was seated next to her.

"I'm Charlotte Kinney and this is my assistant, Lou Smith. We're from the law firm of Larson, Larson and Cohanson and we're here to inform you of the passing of your third cousin, Wilma Cloud, who has left you quite a sizeable inheritance in Frankfurt, Germany."

Barbara was wearing her gold wig and large, signature burgundy sunglasses while Harry had on a short, black shoulder-length wig

Barbara had purchased for him before their last unofficial investigation.

"My *third* cousin, you say?" Dean grimaced.

"I don't have any cousin that I know of by that name you called."

"You are Dean Robert Paltrow, aren't you?"

"That's right."

"Well, according to these documents I have here in my hand…" She raised slightly a manila envelope stacked with papers she usually kept in the car. "…you are entitled to the sum of four hundred thousand dollars cash."

"What did you say?" Dean's eyes widened to the size of golf balls. He was a rough-looking character with dark hair and brown eyes, and couldn't have weighed more than one hundred and sixty pounds.

"You heard right," Barbara said.

Harry was nodding.

"Yeah. I think I remember Cousin Velma," Dean said.

"Wilma's the name," Barbara corrected him.

"Yeah—*Wilma*. I met her once when I was around five years old and later on, the talk was she moved to Germany to start a new life or somethin'. She actually left money for me?"

"She actually did." Barbara nodded. "And it's all yours whenever you get out of prison."

Dean seemed confused and even worried. "Well, I'll be outta here soon."

"How so?" Barbara asked. "We understand you're charged with armed robbery and murder or something of the sort."

He sighed heavily. "Yeah, but I'm innocent of the charges and it's just a matter of time before they let me outta this dump. The most I did was drive the getaway car."

Barbara arched her eyebrow. "I must point out to you, Mr. Paltrow, that if you're not released within forty-five days, your inheritance will instead be handed over to the state."

"No. You can't do that! I have a girl at home that can really use that money even if I'm not able to."

"I'm sorry. It doesn't work that way," Barbara said.

The man seemed deflated.

She glanced at Harry, then faced Dean again. "You know… I would really hate to see this money transferred to the state instead of getting it in the hands of people who need it. What if we try and help you out—with your case, I mean? Seeing that we're attorneys, maybe we can use our skills to help investigate your matter. Sounds like something you might be interested in?"

"Oh, sure!" He quickly replied. "Anything that'll help me get outta here, I'm all for."

"Well, let's begin with you explaining what happened to get you in this jam in the first place. And just so you know—nothing's off limits. We're prepared to bend a few rules if it will help to get that inheritance in your hand."

Dean Paltrow started singing like a bird. It only took the promise of money to get him to even sell out his friends, Rick and Ben.

"They came up with the idea that we should rob a bank and I told them I wouldn't have no part of it. So, they said they'd recruit a guy named Alan Danzabar, an old school mate of ours and see if he's interested in stepping up."

"Alan Danzabar?" Barbara scribbled the name on one of the many blank sheets of paper in her manila envelope.

"Yeah. He lives over there on Kimley Lane with his elderly folks."

"You said you all attended school together?" she asked.

"Yeah. Brass Harbor Middle school."

"So, were your friends successful in recruiting this Alan fellow?"

"Sure! He didn't hesitate, according to what I was told. Even set the whole plan up about how they should pull it off and said he'd been in that bank dozens of times and knew the front area like the back of his hand. Sounded good to me, so I said it just might work and agreed to be the getaway driver. We were gonna make a clean escape." He paused. "The guy wasn't so bright academically—none of us were, come to think of it—but he was a genius otherwise."

"If he was such a genius, why did you all get caught?"

"He was a genius because he managed to get away while the rest of us got caught," he replied.

"How'd that happen?" Barbara pressed.

He left us—that's why. Guess when he heard the sirens, he decided to take off and leave us to try and escape on foot. That was how we got caught. Our legs couldn't outrun those squad cars that were coming from all directions."

"I thought you said you were the getaway driver?"

"I said I *agreed* to be the getaway driver, but that little detail in the plan changed at the last minute. Alan said he'd be the getaway driver and that he'd park in a spot where he knew there would be no camera footage, and we were to follow his instructions to the T, which we did."

"And what about the security guard?" Barbara was curious.

"That wasn't a part of the plan," Dean said. "Things got outta control when the guy locked the doors with the blasted keys and tried to keep us from getting out. I guess he knew the cops were on their way and decided to risk his life doing a dumb thing like that to protect the bank's money. How stupid can a person be?"

Barbara listened quietly.

"We kept telling him to give us the keys, but he refused. Rick Santos, scared to get caught by the cops, panicked and shot the guy, then grabbed the keys and opened the door. After that, we ran out and before we knew it, we took off in different directions because Alan sped off and left us."

"I see." Barbara sighed. "What a story."

"What? You don't believe me?" Dean asked.

"Can you prove what you said is true?"

"Rick Santos and Ben Johnson will verify everything I've said."

"Is that all you've got in terms of proof— *your word*?" Barbara countered.

He thought for a moment. "Actually—no, it isn't. I still have the sketch Alan drew out for us."

"A sketch?" Barbara frowned. "How will that prove what you said is the truth and that this Alan man was involved?"

"Because Alan drew it which means it should have his fingerprints. Shouldn't it?"

Barbara looked Harry's way, then back at Dean.

"Where can we find this so-called proof?" She asked him.

"We used to meet to discuss the heist in an abandoned shack near the river about a mile from the apartment where I live. The sketch is in a shoe box on the top shelf. I can give you directions," he replied.

Barbara liked the sound of that. "I'm listening."

He gave her directions to the shack and she quickly jotted them down.

"Have you mentioned this to anyone else?" she asked.

"I told a reporter yesterday that I have evidence that Alan Danzabar was the mastermind behind the whole thing, but I didn't tell her what that evidence was."

"Why not? And come to think of it, why didn't you tell the police where this so-called evidence was in the first place?"

He was silent for a while, then said, "Because my girl, Melony's fingerprints would be all over it too and I'm not trying to involve her in any of this because she had nothing to do with it. I just showed the sketch to her and explained what the plan was, and she held it to study it more closely. That's pretty much the size of it. Look... there's nothing I wouldn't do for that girl, including taking a bullet for her if the opportunity presented itself, so that's why I haven't told nobody about this, especially the cops. Mel and I have been together for five years and she's a good woman."

Barbara wasn't sure of what to think. His story sounded convincing and so did Alan's. But the fact was, from all accounts, no one, other than those arrested, had placed Alan at the scene of the crime.

She assumed a more comfortable position in the chair and looked him dead in the eyes.

"Mr. Paltrow, even if what you said to me is true pertaining to Alan Danzabar's involvement, it doesn't negate the fact that you are still guilty of the crime. As far as your inheritance is concerned, it doesn't matter if he was there or not. You were still a participant in the robbery during which a security guard was killed. You admitted you were there; others can confirm that fact and whether you pulled the trigger or not, you're just as culpable as the one who did. That's the law. And in light of that fact, there is no chance you will be acquitted of this crime which means that your inheritance is in jeopardy. If, *by some miracle*, you are let off the hook within forty-five days, we'll be in touch."

She gave Harry the nod, hung up the phone and they both got up to leave.

"Hey, wait! That's it?" Dean was confused.

"I'm afraid so," Barbara said. "I truly wish there was more we could do to help you.

But unfortunately, our hands are tied. All the best to you with your case, Mr. Paltrow."

They walked off.

"Wait! There must be some way for me to get the cash. Hey!"

Barbara and Harry were down the corridor and could still hear Dean shouting behind them begging for the money.

Harry shook his head on their way to the car. "His mere freedom is at stake and he's worried about money. It's no surprise to me that he robbed a bank."

"Exactly," Barbara replied. "And can you believe how quickly he remembered his fictitious Cousin Wilma when he heard he'd inherited her estate?"

Harry laughed. "That was funny."

Barbara unlocked the car using the keyless remote.

After they got in and removed their wigs, Harry asked. "So, what do you think of his version of events pertaining to the robbery?"

"I don't know. What I do know is that we need to get a hold of that sketch he went on about," she replied.

"And do what with it?"

"Get it fingerprinted, of course!"

"And how, pray tell, do you suppose we'll get that done?"

"By any means necessary."

She started the engine.

5

The directions Dean gave to the shack could not be plainer. Barbara pulled up alongside a rusty fence and from there she and Harry could see the river at the back of the property. They got out of the car and looked ahead at the dilapidated edifice and the surrounding vacant land. No other buildings were in sight.

"Some people will meet anywhere to devise ungodly deeds," Barbara stated, lowering her shades.

"Yep. Amazing how they found this place practically in the middle of nowhere. No standards." Harry replied. "None at all."

"Okay. Time to get cracking. You stay here and be on the lookout. And I'll go inside to try and find the sketch."

"Similar to how Dean said Alan's role was, huh?" Harry replied, sarcastically.

"Yep. Pretty much. You've got your cell on you, right?"

"Yup. Right here in my pocket." He patted the pocket of his pants.

"Perfect! Give me a ring if anyone shows up."

Harry grimaced. "Why on earth would anyone show up out here?"

She gave him the *don't be stupid look.* "We did. Didn't we?"

"Oh, right!"

Barbara pushed open the gate and hurried over to the little shack situated approximately sixty feet from the front of the property. The building was literally falling apart; the front door lower hinge was barely holding the door in place and when Barbara pulled it open, it became partially detached.

"Whoa!" she said, upon stepping inside. Although it was fairly dark, a bit of sunlight had boldly made its way through several crevices of the wooden structure. Trash was scattered all over the floor: chip bags, beer bottles and faded candy bar wrappings.

"This is so gross!" she muttered, then quickly focused her attention on the row of shelves against the wall at the far back, directly behind a dusty, large, rectangular table. Three iron chairs stood haphazardly around the table on top of which a small, red, tattered notebook was seen next to a Bromeline Sweet Treats cake box.

Barbara went over and opened the lid of the box. Scooping up some slightly hardened crumbs from the inside edge and putting it up to her nose, she quietly said, "Hmmm…pumpkin spice." Then grinned. "I can't imagine a bunch of criminals coming together, eating pumpkin spice cake and planning a bank robbery. Weeeird!"

She closed the lid, wiped her finger on the outside of the cake box and picked up the notebook.

Skimming through the lined pages, she came across just one with writing on it—large numbers scribbled in pencil: 3400 and 520 written underneath it. Having no idea as to what significance those numbers had, she tossed the book back on the table, then headed over to the shelves.

Barbara was five feet seven inches tall, but still had to tiptoe to reach the white shoebox she'd instantly spotted on the top shelf. She finally grabbed it and removing the lid, saw a single folded paper on the inside.

"Bingo!" she blurted.

It was then that she remembered to slip on the clear plastic gloves she'd stashed in her brassiere. Afterwards, she retrieved the paper and opened it up.

"Wow...whoever drew this paid close attention to detail. It's amazing the whole thing wasn't pulled off without a hitch," she muttered.

She folded the paper again, then headed for the door when suddenly, a thought crossed her mind.

"Evidence!" she softly exclaimed. "Can't leave anything that would point back to me being here." She went and snatched the notebook, as well the cake box on which she'd wiped her finger clean, then ran out of the shack and found Harry just where she'd left him—on the side of the car.

"Found it?" he asked.

"Yeah." She hurried over to the driver's side. "Let's go."

"What have you got there?" he said after they got in the car.

"Here's the sketch and this is garbage." She handed everything to him.

"Really? You brought an empty cakebox out of there? Why would you do that?"

"My fingerprints are on it, so I decided to bring the evidence along," she explained.

"So, you didn't put on the gloves before you touched anything?"

"I forgot."

"You do know that your prints would be on the door too, right?" he pointed out.

"I'm not concerned about that," she replied. "It's an old, dilapidated place. Any number of people could've checked it out just being curious."

"You're right," Harry agreed, when another thought struck him. "You do also know you handed the sketch to me and now my fingerprints are on it, right?"

He proceeded to take a look at it.

"Oh! Shucks!" She sighed. "Anyway, it's not like we're turning it over as evidence or anything."

"We're not?"

"Nope. In case Dean Paltrow was telling the truth about his girlfriend, I wouldn't want to…"

"So, you're protecting the girlfriend who might or might not have been involved in planning the bank robbery?"

"He seemed sincere, Harry. He didn't turn over this sketch from the beginning because he's trying to protect her and at the same time entrusted us with this information. How can we betray his trust?" she said.

"Whatever you think is best, Barbara," Harry rolled his eyes.

Although Harry was younger, he was definitely more street smart and was not as ready to take a person's word for anything as Barbara apparently was, particularly when someone managed to hit her soft spot.

"Do you realize how detailed this sketch is—even the numbered steps at the bottom?" he said.

"Same thing I was thinking."

"Whoever drew this must've just sat in the lobby and studied the inside of that bank. Wait! Did you notice the location of the cameras are even on here?"

Barbara glanced over at the sketch. "I don't think I did."

"Certain offices in the front area are also drawn—the manager's here," he pointed. "Assistant manager, there..."

"That job had to have been in the making for a while. It definitely wasn't done on a whim."

Barbara stopped at the first commercial dumpster she spotted. She reached over and grabbed a napkin from the glove compartment and gave it to Harry.

"What's this for?" he asked.

"Wipe off the box, then dump everything, except the sketch, of course," she replied.

"Why wipe off the box?"

"Just do it, Harry."

"The book too?"

"If you want. Here—you might as well dump these too." She slipped off the gloves and handed them to him.

"The whole idea about using gloves was a complete waste of time. Wasn't it?" he remarked.

Barbara ignored the question.

He got out of the car, quickly dumped the items and hurried back, saying nothing. He couldn't figure Barbara out most of the time, despite how long they'd worked together and had become good friends. Barbara's train of thought was usually a mystery to him, but he liked her spunk and her willingness to go the extra mile in search of the truth and justice. He intended to go to law school someday and hopefully, to work side by side with Jack Wilfred, his idol. Wilfred had no idea that Harry looked up to him that much.

Just as they were pulling off, Barbara's cell phone rang.

She sucked her teeth when she saw the caller ID. "Mary's calling," she told Harry. "Wonder what she wants."

"Hi, Mary," she answered on speakerphone.

"Where are you guys?" Mary asked.

"Out west. What's the matter?"

"It's twelve-fifteen. I have to go to lunch in like fifteen minutes. Obviously, no one is here to relieve me."

"Okay. Well, we won't make it there before you have to leave because we have one more stop to make."

"We do?" Harry asked.

"So, if you can't hold on, lock the office and go to lunch, Mary. We'll be there soon."

"Is Mr. Wilfred aware that the office may be locked during regular business hours?" Mary responded. "This is not regular practice here at J. Wilfred and Co."

"Don't get beside yourself, Mary Grisham. Might I remind you who's in charge while Mr. Wilfred's away? And can you think of why it is he always leaves me in charge and not you?"

There was a brief pause on the line.

"It's because I'm the *paralegal slash administrator* like you pointed out ever-so-clearly and you're the receptionist. You take care of the phone calls and welcome the guests when they come in and do a little paperwork. That's all you need to be concerned about. Leave the running of the office to me, okay?"

"I hear you."

Barbara hung up the phone.

"That woman is more than a pain in the butt. She's a boil!"

Harry laughed.

"*Is Mr. Wilfred aware that the office may be locked during regular business hours?*" She mocked. "What does she care?"

"Do you know you're even cuter when you get angry?" he said.

"You're full of crap, Harry."

Barbara tried to calm herself down as she drove. Mary was getting on her last nerve and she wasn't sure how much more of her *lip* she could take.

"So, where's the next stop you mentioned?" Harry asked.

"Ian," she replied.

"Ian—the *cop slash forensic guy*?"

"Yep."

"What for?"

"To check for Alan's fingerprints on that sketch," she said.

"Okay—that's your friend. Will be interesting to see how that unfolds especially how you're not officially or unofficially turning this sketch over to the police."

"Leave it to me, Harry Buford. Leave it to me."

"I certainly will, Barbara Sandosa."

6

"Are you out of your mind, Barbara?" Ian Roberts barked.

He and Barbara were standing in front of her car in the parking lot of the police forensic lab where he worked.

"Look...I called you out here for a simple favor, Ian. You know we go way back."

"But you're asking me to secretly fingerprint a document that should have been collected by the police and entered into evidence in the first place. This sketch is supposedly linked to a crime, Barbara! A crime in which a guy was killed. How can you expect me to check for fingerprints without letting anyone here know about it? Are you trying to get me fired or worse, arrested?"

"You know I'd never intentionally put you in jeopardy, Ian," Barbara replied. "Wasn't I there for you when your mom was on her dying bed? Didn't I come over every day with hot soup and herbal tea to help keep up her strength? I've known you all my life, Ian—from when we were toddlers. My parents and your parents were best friends. Can't you do this one favor for me? I promise, it will be just between us."

Ian glanced at Harry in the passenger seat.

"Harry doesn't count," she quickly said. "You know he'd never squeal."

Ian sighed deeply. "So, what if this Alan Danzabar guy's prints show up on this sketch? You still won't turn it over?"

She shook her head. "I don't know. That's a bridge I'll have to cross when I get there."

"Why the reluctance though? Are you protecting someone else, Barbara?"

She looked away from him and Ian's answer was clear.

"Who is it this time, huh? Who's supposedly the innocent victim?"

"Just check for Alan's fingerprints. That's all," she replied. "And call me the minute you're done. His fingerprints should be in the database, right?"

"I'll have to see. These days, fingerprints are required in order to get certain government-issued documentation, so…"

"Yep. Okay. Thanks a lot, Ian. I really appreciate it."

"I know." He nodded, sliding the sketch into the pocket of his shirt.

Ian was a middle-aged bachelor and also a *Momma's boy* who still lived in the same house he grew up in. Barbara had always thought he and his late mother's connection was more like a chokehold on Ian since Mrs. Roberts refused to let him use the proverbial wings. Every romantic interest he ever had was chased off eventually by the lonely widow by means of some grievous thought she'd put into his head or by some doubt she'd planted about the girl's intention. Ian always listened to his mother and was totally devastated when she passed away five years earlier. Almost drank himself into rehab and out of a job, but finding the right counselor seemed to steer him in the right direction. It took the better part of two years for him to accept the fact that his mother was gone and that he needed to continue to live, and Barbara was there for him every step of the way.

As Ian headed back to work, Barbara got into the car.

"Well, that was heavy," Harry said.

"I hate to put him in such a position, but I don't have a choice," she replied. "We need to know who's telling the truth—Alan Danzabar or Dean Paltrow and the others. Mr. Wilfred's good name is at stake here. We can't have any reservations as to who he's taken on as a client."

Harry quietly nodded.

Barbara started the car and they headed back to the office.

By the time they arrived at the office, Mary was getting out of her little brown hatchback. Barbara pulled into her own parking space next to Mary's car and she and Harry got out.

"I thought you two would've been back already!" Mary exclaimed as she headed to the front door, keys jingling in her hand.

"Had a good lunch, Mary?" Barbara asked, ignoring her statement.

"I surely did."

Harry was carrying two Charlie Jigs Fried Chicken bags while Barbara held the cold drinks in the cardboard holder. They'd stopped off at Charlie's, two blocks away, for lunch and decided to eat at the office.

"No more dieting for you, huh, Harry?" Mary smiled as she unlocked the front door.

"I threw that dieting stuff out the window weeks ago. Haven't you noticed?" he replied with a matching smile.

"Actually—yes, I have! I figured you might've gained a few pounds over the past couple of weeks."

She opened the door and allowed them to enter first.

"Thank you," Barbara said, passing her.

"Thanks," Harry muttered.

"We'll be in the kitchen if you need us," Barbara told Mary.

"I figured as much." Mary headed to her desk.

"That's a low blow she threw at you out there," Barbara said to Harry at the lunch table.

He'd just taken a bite out of his fried chicken thigh. "Mary'll be just fine. A few pounds packed on over a couple of weeks ain't bad. I can always lose the weight, but she's stuck with that ugly face of hers."

Barbara nearly choked on her fries. "I didn't think she was *that* bad-looking!"

"You are overdue for a new prescription for those glasses you hardly ever wear," he commented. "Like I said, Mary'll be just fine."

Harry lived with his aged father who had raised him as a single dad after Harry's mother passed away when he was just six years old. The two had a close relationship and Harry often spoke about how his dad tried to fill the void in his life by being involved in everything he ever took part in. Especially keeping him busy with music lessons, sports and a host of other activities that his father felt would have made him well rounded. However, as much as his dad tried to fill the void, Harry realized it was still always there and he felt it every time he looked at photographs of his mother that were in several places throughout the house. Some were snapshots of the three of them together while others were of just her or of her and Harry. He remembered her smile, her voice, her scent and swore sometimes when he opened the door of the house that a whiff sailed right past his nose. Katrina Melony Buford was a special lady who lived in his heart and whose love he'd always felt. There was something about Barbara that reminded him of his mother. They did have similar features, especially the dark, wavy hair and brown eyes. Subconsciously, he felt the motherly connection to Barbara is what prevented him from saying no to all the risky stunts she ever pulled.

Mary appeared at the door. "Hilda Rubenstein is here to see Mr. Wilfred and she doesn't seem to understand that he can't be reached at the moment."

"What is her problem this time?" Barbara asked, putting down her soft drink.

"She and Mr. Rubenstein are now fighting over who would keep Skippy, the dog, and the madam wants Mr. Wilfred to schedule a meeting right away with her husband's attorney to sort it out."

"She can't be serious," Barbara said.

"She's serious." She shrugged. "I'm gonna tell her you'll be out in a second to speak with her." And she left.

Barbara looked at Harry. "You know what I can't understand?"

"What?" he asked.

"How Mr. Rubenstein put up with that woman for twenty years. It's amazing he didn't file for divorce a long time ago. She's impossible sometimes!"

"And totally delusional," Harry added. That's what money does to you sometimes."

Barbara wiped her mouth, threw the napkin into the trash and headed out front.

Hilda Rubenstein was sitting in the reception area with her legs crossed. She was a fifty-year-old natural blonde with expensive taste and flawless features—partially with the help of cosmetic surgery. She was wearing a light red silk dress which fell below her knees and a deep red scarf. And as usual, she was holding a lit cigarette securely between her fingers.

"Mrs. Rubenstein, how are you today?" Barbara put on a cheerful face.

"I'm not here to discuss how I'm doing. I'm here to see Mr. Wilfred," Hilda answered, taking a puff of her cigarette.

"Do you mind putting that out please?" Barbara frankly stated.

"As a matter of fact, I do mind."

"Mrs. Rubenstein, must we go through this every time? You know the rules. No smoking is allowed inside the office."

She sighed deeply. "Okay."

Mary reached for the ashtray that's usually kept in her drawer. She then handed it to Barbara and Barbara gave it to Hilda who then used it to put out her cigarette. They had made those exact steps multiple times.

"Happy?" Hilda forced a smile as she gave Barbara the ashtray.

"Thank you," Barbara replied. "Now, you were asking for Mr. Wilfred. Unfortunately, he's out of town at the moment. Is there anything I can help you with?"

"That *out of town* talk isn't going to wash with me! I pay him handsomely to do a job and that is precisely what I expect! He isn't answering my calls, so you need to get a hold of him and tell him he needs to get back here right away because it's urgent."

Inside, Barbara was hoping that the floor would open and swallow up the cantankerous woman.

"What exactly is the matter, Mrs. Rubenstein?"

"I explained that to this woman already!" She pointed at Mary, who dared not respond to her.

"Well, I'm asking you now," Barbara said.

"It's Skippy. Luther's trying to take her from me. He already has our daughter, Kate, living with him. Why take Skippy away from me too?"

"Kate made the decision to live with her father, Mrs. Rubenstein. She's twenty years old, which means she's of age."

"Did I need you to tell me that?" Hilda snarled.

"I guess you didn't. Well... as far as your dog is concerned, Mr. Wilfred will have to contact you when he gets back."

"And when is that supposed to be?"

"In two days," Barbara replied.

"But what if Luther sneaks onto the property and kidnaps Skippy while I'm asleep? Or what if he convinces the police to barge into the house and take her from me? Something has to be done to prevent that from happening!"

She seemed terrified of the very thought.

"For all it's worth, Mrs. Rubenstein, considering Mr. Rubenstein's past behavior, I highly doubt that you need to worry about any of those scenarios, especially the first."

She abruptly stood up. "Are you suggesting that my soon-to-be ex-husband has been conducting himself in a civil manner, Ms. Sandosa, and that I don't?"

"I am not suggesting that," Barbara replied. "Look—upon Mr. Wilfred's return to office, I will relay your concern to him and he'll give you a call, okay?"

"You said he'll be back in two days?" Hilda asked.

"Yes, that's when he's expected." Barbara's wide smile won the fight over the frown that was itching to emerge.

"Okay. But I'll remind you, Ms. Sandosa, that I have paid a lot of money to this law firm and expect to be treated better than most. You let Mr. Wilfred know the moment he calls to check in here."

"I'll do that." Barbara nodded.

Hilda headed for the door.

"You have a good day now," Barbara told her while handing Mary the ashtray.

After Hilda was gone, Harry—who'd returned from the kitchen a couple of minutes earlier—Barbara, and Mary all had a good chuckle.

"The nerve of that woman!" Mary exclaimed, tossing the contents of the ashtray into the trash bin.

"She's one of those people who suddenly felt entitled after they got lucky and married into money." Harry sat at his desk. "You'd think she was born with a gold spoon in her mouth."

Barbara headed for her desk too. "Every time she comes in here, there's some kind of drama. She's toxic—that's what!"

"Yep," Mary agreed.

Barbara logged on to her computer and opened a file folder in front of her.

"Aren't you gonna finish your lunch?" Harry asked.

"That woman killed my appetite. Will take it home and finish it for dinner," she said.

"Okey dokey." Harry then went about his duties.

---

arbara loved the kitchen and especially the oven. Not just on weekends when she had more time to prepare her favorite recipes, but also throughout the week. On Thursday night, she cooked a large pot of pea soup and dumpling—a recipe she'd been given by a lady she met on a Caribbean cruise a decade earlier. The woman, whom Barbara had quickly befriended—in the restroom of all places, happened to be a chef aboard the cruise ship. For the remaining six days of the cruise, they got to know each other, exchanged recipes, since they both loved to cook, and phone numbers. Claudia Jenson became one of Barbara's best friends.

Claudia was a black woman who lived on an island named Andros in The Bahamas. She had two teenage children, Renee and Ronisha, and was married to Ron, a fisherman. Barbara got to meet the whole family once after Claudia invited her down for a visit and Barbara admired how well they all got along. Spending a few days with Claudia and her family made her feel like she was missing out on so much as a single woman living alone and she happened to express that to her new friend the day before she left for home.

"Not everyone was meant to get married, Barb," she recalled Claudia telling her as they sat together on a park bench. "Many people are single and have a wonderful life. I admire how you can pick up and go places whenever you want without having to think of other responsibilities first. And you have wonderful friends, neighbors, a great job and a caring boss. Just because you live alone doesn't mean you are alone."

Those words hit home to Barbara in a powerful way. In fact, Claudia's viewpoint made her appreciate the life she had so much more and to see it from a completely different perspective. It didn't mean from time to time when she saw families together that she still didn't wish she had one of her own, but seeing them certainly didn't make her feel deprived or that she was lacking.

After cooking the soup, Barbara went to take a small pot over to her neighbors, the Shelbys. It was just after seven o'clock when she stepped onto the porch of their white, single storey, three-bedroom house and rang the doorbell.

Moments later, Janet opened the door.

"Barbara! How good it is to see you!" she said.

"Hi, Janet. I just made some soup and thought I'd bring a pot over for you and Ralph. I hope you haven't had dinner yet."

"I'm afraid we just ate, but it can always come in handy tomorrow." She smiled. "Please come in."

Barbara went in and immediately spotted their cat Ralphy lying on the piano in the living room. He was a large Ragdoll with silky soft white and light grey fur with the most gorgeous blue eyes and cutest pink nostrils she'd ever seen. The thought had once crossed Barbara's mind that if there was a feline show in Grenhurst, Ralphy should definitely be a contestant as she was sure he'd emerge the winner.

"Hi, Ralphy!" she petted the cat.

"I'll take that," Janet offered, reaching for the pot of soup. "So nice of you to think of us!"

107

"It's nothing," Barbara replied as Janet headed to the kitchen.

Ralph Shelby was sitting in his wheelchair watching television. He had developed dementia a year earlier and some days did not recognize Janet, Ralphy, or even remembered who he was.

That night, Barbara could tell that he was not really *there* with them as he gazed toward the TV screen.

She went over to him and rested her hand on his shoulder. "Good night, Ralph. How are ya?"

He looked up at her. "Hey…hey. Doing okay."

Barbara was glad to hear him respond.

"I brought some pea soup for you and Janet. You always said you love my pea soup." She smiled.

Janet walked in and sat on the couch. She gestured for Barbara to come join her.

"Honestly, he's not really been doing that well," Janet whispered loudly as Barbara sat next to her.

"I'm really sorry to hear that," Barbara replied. "It's amazing how people you know and love can be transformed by such a disease."

"Yes indeed. I miss the old him. Sometimes, he's in good spirits and remembers who Ralphy and I are, but other times…"

Barbara patted Janet's knee. "I understand."

"He was my prince charming when we were young and in love, and he still is today fifty years later."

The words brought a smile to Barbara's face. "That's so sweet," she said. "Somewhere there inside even when he's not quite himself, he's loving you just as much. All you can do is be here for him like you've always been."

"You're right. Thank you for your kind words, Barb."

Janet and Ralph were always a warm, loving couple. Janet was far more talkative than her husband was and sometimes, in Barbara's opinion, talked a bit too much. However, she was a good person and never meant any harm to anyone.

"I'd better be going now. Just came to drop off the soup and wish you both a good night." Barbara started to get up.

"Thank you, dear. I can't wait to have a big, old helping of it tomorrow. Ralphy always loves your soup."

Barbara told Ralph she was leaving, then Janet walked with her to the door.

"Have a good night, dear!" Janet waved goodbye as Barbara walked off.

* * * *

"Good morning! Good morning!" Barbara said the following day at work. "Who's up for pea soup today?"

"You don't mean pea soup and dough?" Mary's eyes widened.

Mary rarely ever ate anything that Barbara brought into the office, but did try the pea soup and dumpling once and was hooked ever since.

"Oh, yes!" Barbara continued on towards the kitchen with Mary and Harry eagerly following behind.

"I'm not waiting for lunch this time," Harry noted in the kitchen. "The last time I made that mistake Mary here helped herself to more than her fair share. So, I'll be having mine for breakfast."

"No, I did not!" Mary retorted. "I believe that last time you actually came back for seconds."

"That's a boldfaced lie and you know it, Mary!" Harry said.

"Now, now, people…there's enough here for everyone," Barbara happily interjected.

"What is it this time?" Wilfred walked in.

"Pea soup and dumpling, sir," Harry answered.

"Oh, great."

"Good morning, Mr. Wilfred," Barbara said. "I do believe this pot is big enough this time."

"We'll see soon enough," he replied. "When you're done in here, Barbara, I'd like to see you in my office for a briefing."

"Sure thing, sir."

Harry and Mary went straightaway to dish up a bowl of soup while Barbara followed Wilfred to his office. She made a detour to her desk first where she rested her purse in its usual spot and her cell phone on top of the desk.

Ten minutes after her meeting with Wilfred ended, her cell phone vibrated and she quickly picked up after noticing it was Ian calling.

"Can you talk?" he asked.

"Yeah. Shoot." She pressed her phone against her ear.

"The results were negative for your guy," he said. "Can you swing by my place after work?"

"Sure. What time?"

"I'm on an early shift today, so I'll be home by four. Any time you're free after that is fine."

"Okay, will do. Thanks."

She ended the call.

"You're not having any soup?" Harry asked.

"I'll have a little for lunch," Barbara replied. "Had a bagel before I left home." She then leaned over and said in a lowered voice, "That was Ian."

"Really? What'd he say?" Harry drew closer.

"Alan's fingerprints aren't on the sketch. It just proves that Dean Paltrow must've been lying about him being involved, just like he said."

"Well, that's good to know. Case closed then."

"It's crazy to think someone would just randomly accuse another person of being involved in something they clearly had no part in. I don't understand why those men would do something like that." Barbara sat back in her chair and placed her hand beneath her chin.

"Maybe it's jealousy," Harry said. "Alan has a steady job; seems to be a good father and is just living life the best way he could. Sometimes, that's enough to make people jealous, you know?"

She sighed. "I guess. They were obviously trying to ruin this guy's life. Well, he's in good hands with Mr. Wilfred. If anything ever comes up, he need not worry about having the best legal representation out there."

"I second that," Harry said. "What about the sketch?"

"What about it?"

"Ian's not keeping it, right?"

"Oh, right! No, he's not. I'm going by his place after work to pick it up."

"And then what?"

She gave him that confused look.

"What are you gonna do with it?" he pressed.

She thought for a moment. "I'm not sure yet. I'll shove it in my nightstand drawer until I decide."

He grimaced. "You're gonna keep evidence related to a crime in your nightstand drawer? Are you sure you work for a law firm?"

"It'll be all right. I'll get rid of it soon enough."

Barbara arrived at Ian's house at a quarter past five. He looked like he'd just woken up.

"Did I interrupt your sleep?" Barbara asked, walking in.

"No, not at all. Just had a nap; got up a few minutes ago," Ian smoothed his hair back. "Have a seat."

Ian's mother had OCD and she kept the place spotless. He had to fall in line with keeping things just the way she wanted them and often felt her wrath whenever he happened to slip up. Barbara recalled those days being there and witnessing the eyerolling drama. Mrs. Roberts often calmed down pretty quickly after telling him a piece of her mind because Ian truly was her heartstring—the reason she lived.

Since her passing, he obviously hadn't let her down since the house was pretty much in the same condition she'd kept it. And Ian, as far as Barbara knew, didn't have OCD.

"Here's the sketch." He handed it to her, then sat on the sofa.

"Thanks a lot." She stuffed it in the inside pocket of her purse.

"I was wondering if you heard about the missing cash from the bank robbery?" he said.

"I thought they recovered the money when they nabbed the robbers." Barbara was surprised by the question.

"They recovered some of it. It wasn't publicized, but a duffle bag stashed with cash— the sum of two hundred and fifty thousand is still out there somewhere."

"What?"

"Yep. I was just wondering if you knew that."

"Nope. I had no idea."

He got up and started pacing. "I assume this Alan guy is Jack Wilfred's client. Am I right?"

"Yeah…" Barbara was starting to wonder where the conversation was going.

"Did you know Mrs. Arinthia Danzanbar, his mother, paid Dean Paltrow a visit yesterday?"

"In jail?" She arched her brows.

"Yep. Had a fairly short conversation from what I heard. Since then, Dean suddenly

118

went silent when it came to all that talk about Alan being involved," he said.

"Really?"

"Uh-huh."

Barbara was suddenly deep in thought.

"What are you thinking?" He sat down again.

"I'm thinking that I need to find out why our client's mother paid a visit to one of the guys who accused her son of being an accomplice to a serious crime," she replied.

"I'd think the reason is because she wanted to ask him to stop calling her son's name," Ian replied. "Maybe she had enough of it and decided to take the matter into her own hands. Although I must admit, it's kind of weird for an elderly woman to have to stand up for her grown son like that who can pretty much stand on his own two feet."

Barbara heard him talking, but she could clearly envision Ian's mother doing the exact same thing on his behalf had the shoe been on the other foot. Obviously, he wasn't thinking clearly.

She got up. "I don't know."

"You're leaving already?" He stood up too.

"Yep. Gotta make a stop to the store on the way home. Look…thanks for everything, Ian. You're a sweetheart." She kissed him on the cheek, then headed for the door.

He stood in the doorway and watched until she got in her car.

* * * *

After driving away, Barbara quickly retrieved her cell phone from her purse and dialed Harry's number.

"What's up?" he answered on the first ring.

"Be ready tomorrow evening at six. I'm coming to pick you up."

"For what? Tomorrow's Saturday—my day off, remember?"

"Just be ready. There's been a recent development," she said.

"Okay."

Barbara was about to hang up.

"Hey! How should I dress?" he asked.

"I don't care what you wear, Harry."

"Uh—oh."

"Uh—oh, what?"

"I'm not gonna like this, am I?" he asked.

"Neither of us will, but it has to get done."

She ended the call.

---

9

*T**he following evening…***

Although the office was closed, Barbara swung by and quickly jotted down some directions from a file in the cabinet. Then she drove across town to pick up Harry.

After honking her horn a couple of times in front of the Bufords' house in the suburbs, Harry opened the front door and made his way to the car. He was dressed in a blue tee shirt and white knee-length shorts.

"So what's the plan? he asked her.

"We're going to stake out the Danzabars' place," she replied.

"Are you kidding me, Barbara?"

Refusing to discuss anything about the plan on the phone all day, despite how many times Harry had called, she finally explained to him what Ian had said to her the night before.

"So we're gonna stake out the Danazabars' place, as you say, and what are you hoping to uncover? Alan's supposedly squeaky clean since his fingerprints were not on the sketch, so I don't understand the purpose of this trip."

"I'm not sure I do either. But something's nagging at me that we need to do this. We'll park across the street for a while and just observe."

"Okay...so we'll stay in the car is what you're saying?" He was hopeful.

"Pretty much. Unless we need to get out for a better view."

As he suspected.

"Okay, Barbara. I guess we'll know when we get there."

Alan lived on a ranch-style one acre property with his parents, which consisted of a guest house further back in the yard similar to the way he had described it. The properties on Kimley Lane were fairly large and many of the homes had been standing there for close to a century.

Barbara pulled up across the street from the Danzabar residence where they were able to get a view of the main house up front and the little one at the back where Alan claimed he resided.

"Nice place they have here, despite it being old," Harry commented.

"Yep." Barbara slid her cap over her head.

They were parked parallel to a vacant land where large trees stood near the edge of the property line providing shade from the extended branches. Although they arrived just before six thirty, the sun had not yet set and they were able to see clearly into the yard across the street.

"It's a quiet neighborhood." Barbara tilted her seat back twenty minutes later. By then, dusk was falling rapidly.

"Hey, that looks like our guy!" Harry was peering over at the Danzabar property.

Alan was climbing down a tree house situated a good fifty feet parallel to the little house out back.

"What the hell is a grown man like him doing up in a tree house?" Barbara muttered.

"Weird as hell," Harry remarked. Then on second thought he said, "Maybe that little boy's still in him and he goes up every so often just to relax."

"That's a possibility," Barbara agreed.

They watched him walk over to the main house where a few lights were on and assumed he entered through the back door.

Shortly after he disappeared from sight, they heard some commotion in the house.

"Sounds like arguing, doesn't it?" Harry looked at Barbara.

"Sure does. Let's go check it out."

They both got out of the vehicle and quietly crossed the street. Barbara was relieved that she hadn't seen any dogs in the yard and figured they might not have to worry about being chased off the property.

They crept up to the side of the main house where the sounds were coming from, then peeped inside of a window.

An elderly couple were seated in separate chairs in the living room and Alan was standing near the mantle berating them.

"Why do we always have to go through this?" he said to them. "You two keep this place like a pigsty. I'm the only one who ever lifts a finger around here and I pay all the bills."

The couple took his scolding for another few minutes until the old man spoke up. Both he and his wife looked to be in their eighties.

"Alan, we've let you have your say like always, but might I remind you that we raised and took care of you and paid all the bills around here straight up until we retired. Do you really expect people our age to mop and do housework like we used to? Why are we even arguing over something like that, especially now since you have all that extra cash? You can go right out and hire a housekeeper a couple times a week and stop nagging and tormenting your elderly father and mother."

Barbara and Harry glanced at each other.

"Can't you see how much stress you're putting, especially on your mother?" Russell Danzabar continued. "Don't you care? She takes care of little Trina all day while you're out and about and you don't even appreciate that."

"Leave Trina out of this! She's your grandchild and everyone has to pull their weight. It's not like she has a mom that gives a damn about her," Alan replied.

"Seems to me she doesn't have a dad that gives a damn either," Russell rebutted.

"How dare you, old man!" Alan was enraged. "I take care of my daughter." He scraped the contents of the mantle onto the floor with the back of his arm.

"You're never there for her," Arinthia Danzabar chimed in. "Not as you should be and you're not responsible. You know she's in her room sleeping and you're making all of this noise."

"That child's used to it by now," Russell remarked. "She's heard this raucous over and over again, and just sleeps right through it."

Barbara was shaking her head. As far as she could tell, Alan was not that wonderful guy he portrayed himself to be.

"The guy's a jerk," Harry whispered in disgust. He couldn't imagine ever treating his father the way Alan was addressing his parents.

"Since you went and involved yourself in that bank robbery, you got worse," Russell went on. "That money you got out there is blood money, Alan. A man died because of it!"

"I had nothing to do with that guy getting shot. Rick's an idiot; that was never the plan." He slid his fingers through his hair. "So, what you want me to do, Dad? Turn myself in? Rot in prison like those guys will?"

"No!" his mother exclaimed. "You need to be here for Trina and for us. Like I told you,

Dean agreed to keep his mouth shut once you give a hundred thousand of the money to his girlfriend tomorrow. Just do that and this whole thing will be over with. No one will call your name ever again."

"Well, I don't like any of it," Russell said. "We didn't raise him to be no crook."

"Maybe if you would've been there for me as a father, I would've turned out different," Alan said.

Russell stood up, although it was a bit of a challenge due to his arthritic knees.

"So, it's *my* fault then? I worked my butt off to give you and your mother everything you need. You ungrateful..."

"Stop it, Russell!" his wife shouted. "This carrying on back and forth doesn't make any sense."

Russell gave his son an angry glare, then slowly sat down again.

"Give that girl the money as you agreed, Alan, and this will be over," Arinthia urged.

Alan did a bit of pacing, then he stopped and sighed. "There's no guarantee if I turn over the cash that this will be over, Mom. They can still talk and eventually, the cops could still come and arrest me. So, I decided it's best I take off—go to Mexico or some other country where no one can touch me. I'll leave fifty thousand here for you to help take care of Trina and I'll send more later on."

"That's ridiculous!" Russell yelled. "You'd be looking over your shoulder for the rest of your life!"

"Don't do it, Alan. Just pay the money. I promise everything will be all right," his mother cried.

"I've made up my mind," Alan said, stoically. "And I won't discuss this again."

His parents glanced at each other. Arinthia was clearly heartbroken, and she burst into tears.

"I'm going to check in on Trina," Alan said before heading into the hallway toward the bedroom.

"He's gonna do what he wants and there's nothing we can do to stop him," Russell told his wife. "He's not very loyal to anyone, is he? He betrayed his friends; took off with the cash after one of them tossed it into the car, leaving the guy stranded out there for the cops to nab. Now, he made an agreement to share some of the money, but wants it all for himself. That's the bottom line, Arinthia. That's the boy you cloaked all his life—the monster you raised."

"Shut up, Russell!" She stormed off into the kitchen where she continued sobbing at the table.

"We have to get to that tree house," Barbara whispered to Harry. "Before he comes back outside."

"Okay," Harry replied.

"They scurried over to the rear of the main house and arrived at the tall maple tree with a wooden structure nestled near the top. Fortunately for them, there were strips of thick wood from a foot near the base of the trunk leading straight up to the top.

"I'll climb up. You wait here," Barbara said.

"I should go," Harry replied. "I'm younger."

"And a bit heavier than me. So, I should go."

"Barbara, I'm a master tree climber. We had a tree house at the old place where we lived a few years after mom died and I practically lived in that house. I'll go up and have a look around."

Barbara relented. "Okay, but be careful and hurry up!" She retrieved a mini searchlight from her pocket and handed it to him.

"Thanks." He soon started up the tree. "Hey—what should I do if I find anything?"

"Take it, of course!" she replied.

"Wouldn't that be interfering with evidence?"

"Maybe, but who cares? We need to stop this guy from skipping town with a quarter of a million!"

Barbara kept looking around as Harry made his way up the maple tree. They both were terribly nervous and after seeing Alan Danzanbar in action couldn't wait to get off the property.

Harry got to the top and went into the little tree house. Scanning the inside with the flashlight, he noticed a bench lodged from one side of the structure to the next with two cinder blocks placed side by side beneath it for support. There was nothing more that he could see other than the wooden floor beneath him. He shone the light in multiple directions.

"There's nothing here," he muttered. "Maybe the guy was just enjoying quiet time up here after all."

Then the light hit a corner of the floor beneath the bench. Something was lodged behind one of the cinder blocks. Harry reached in and grabbed it—a black, leather duffle bag, then he looked inside and his eyes widened.

"Holy Moly!" he quietly exclaimed, gazing at the stacks of hundred-dollar bills held tightly together in neat bands.

He zipped it back up, tossed it over his shoulder, shut off the flashlight and proceeded back down the tree house with great speed. As he was about to take the last step, he fell, landing on his buttocks.

Barbara helped him up.

"I found it!" he told her quietly. "I found the cash!"

"Wow," she replied in astonishment.

Suddenly, the back porch came on. "Who's there?" they heard Alan's voice. Then the door opened and he stepped outside.

"Let's get out of here!" Barbara cried.

She and Harry ran as quickly as they could across the yard, passing the main house and heading straight for the road. Alan was on their tail, yelling for them to stop, but for them that request was not an option.

Barbara got to the car first, having unlocked the doors with the remote. She quickly got inside and Harry was in the passenger seat seconds later. Alan was at the edge of his parents' property just about to cross the street when a car whisked by. Barbara started the engine and took off down the street, she and Harry still trying to catch their breath.

"That was a close call!" Harry said. "You think he recognized us?"

"Not a chance," Barbara replied. "It's too dark and that porch light wasn't much use either."

Harry glanced behind them. "You think he's gonna follow us?"

"I doubt it since he couldn't know for sure if we took anything of his in the first place." She slid her cell phone out of her pocket. "I'm calling Mr. Wilfred."

"To tell him what? That we snuck around the Danzabars' property and found the cash?"

"Kind of," she replied. "I'll dress it up a bit."

Jack Wilfred answered a few moments later and Barbara explained that they had suspected Alan might not have been completely honest with him relating to his involvement in the bank robbery. And after staking out the residence, they happened to come across the duffle bag with the cash.

"You *happened* to come across it, huh?" Wilfred replied. "Barbara, you are not a detective or the FBI. You are a paralegal! What are you two doing breaking the law and risking getting hurt or killed by trespassing on other people's property?" He told her to put him on speakerphone, then he gave them both a scolding. Finally, he said, "Go straight to the police station on Fourth Street, ask for Detective Tony Shepard and turn the bag over to him. You'll need to give a statement, of course. And I'll see you two in my office first thing Monday morning!"

He hung up.

"That went well, didn't it?" Harry was being cynical.

"He'll calm down by Monday," Barbara responded.

She drove to the police station and they met with Detective Shepard, a short, stout man in his early sixties. Barbara gave the duffle bag to him.

"I spoke with Jack several minutes ago," he told them. "And I immediately had some cars dispatched to the Danzabar residence."

"I hope Alan didn't get away." Harry worried.

He offered them something to drink, but they declined.

"You two have a lot of nerve doing what you did," he said as they sat in his office. "I must tell you though—but I guess you already know that Jack is quite upset."

"We know," Barbara replied. "He thinks of us as family and Harry and I feel the same way about him. That's why we had to find out the truth about Alan Danzabar. Mr. Wilfred had taken him on as a client and charged him practically *chicken feed* as a retainer out of the goodness of his heart. All he ever asks of his clients is honesty and Alan obviously couldn't give him that."

"Well, I certainly wouldn't encourage you two to play detective anymore because it can be a very dangerous game. If he had a gun, he could've shot you and probably gotten away with it too since you were trespassing on private property."

"I know," Barbara replied.

"The good thing is…you've recovered the bank's money and at the same time you've provided the evidence we needed to arrest Alan Danzabar. We always knew he must have been involved in the robbery. Just didn't have enough evidence to make the arrest sooner, and the D.A. refused to allow us to do so based solely on hearsay."

Barbara and Harry looked at each other and smiled. They each felt a sense of pride in helping to carry out law and justice.

10

F***irst thing Monday morning...***

"As you know by now, they've arrested Alan Danzabar and are charging him with armed robbery and second-degree homicide along with his coconspirators," Wilfred said, standing near his office window.

"Yes, sir," Harry replied.

He and Barbara were sitting next to each other on the other side of Wilfred's desk.

"Serves him right!" Barbara exclaimed. "I heard they're also charging his mother with something."

"They were going to, but Tony said they let her off with a stern warning."

"I can understand that," Harry said, thinking of his own mother and how if she was alive he would've wanted mercy shown to her regardless of what she'd done.

"The guy had the nerve to call me after they arrested him. Of course, I told him he'd need to find another attorney and we'll be refunding his retainer fee."

Wilfred took a seat and looked Barbara and Harry dead in the eyes. "This isn't the first stunt you two pulled. I know you both mean well, but you've got to stop taking matters into your own hands. Let the police do their jobs; that's what they're there for. And for goodness sake, stop thinking you must do all these crazy things to protect me and this firm's reputation! Our reputation will remain intact so long as you two stop getting yourselves into mischief. Am I clear?"

"Yes, sir," they answered.

"That's all for now. Get back to work."

He shook his head as they were leaving and opened Mrs. Rubenstein's file. He intended to consult Mr. Rubenstein's attorney to see if they could reach a satisfactory resolution in the matter of who gets Skippy, the dog.

Mary had a cunning smile on her face when Barbara and Harry were returning to their desks.

"Smirk all you want," Barbara said, "But at least we caught a criminal. What great deed have you done lately?" She proceeded to sit down.

The smile quickly disappeared from Mary's face and she got back to work entering data on the computer.

After Harry sat down, he gave Barbara a high five. "Team work!" he quietly exclaimed.

"Yes indeed," Barbara replied.

* * * *

That night, Barbara was fast asleep when she was awakened by the sound of gunshots, that seemed to come from nearby, specifically where the Shelby's lived. She immediately switched on the lamp, got up and quickly threw on her robe. She had the most awful feeling in the pit of her gut as she swung open her front door and ran toward her neighbors' house. It was just minutes past midnight, and oddly, the light was still on in the Shelby's living room. She knocked on the door and called out to them, but there was no answer.

She thought to check the doorknob, and twisting it, the door creaked open. There, in the living room, she saw the bodies of Ralph and Janet Shelby. Ralph was slumped over in his favorite chair in front of the television and Janet was lying on her back on the couch with one hand dangling over the edge, and a small handgun on the floor beneath her hand. Ralphy was on the chair with Janet, licking her face.

"Oh my God!" Barbara exclaimed.

She went in and immediately got Ralphy. "Oh my. You poor cat." She snuggled him.

Other neighbors started to come out of their houses and were shocked to find the beloved Shelbys deceased by means of what appeared to be a murder-suicide.

"Someone, call the police!" Barbara cried. She was heartbroken to think that perhaps, Janet Shelby had been planning this tragedy all along.

~ The End ~

Is the death of Ralph and Janet Shelby as cut and dry as it seems? Or will Barbara Sandosa uncover something that no one would have ever suspected? Get ready for book two in this exciting series:

Red Velvet & Murder

Order your copy today.

And if you've enjoyed this book, please be so kind to leave your review online.

ANOTHER COZY MYSTERY SERIES YOU'RE SURE TO ENJOY!

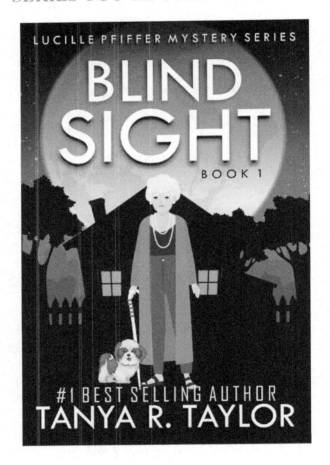

FREE EXCERPT:

1

Super Vanilla

I carefully descended the air-conditioned jitney and started down the sidewalk with my cane in hand and Nilla, my pet Shih Tzu on leash at my side. Taking a cab was our preferred mode of transport, but sometimes we enjoyed a nice, long bus ride instead. Nestled on both sides of the street were a number of shops, including convenience stores, jewelry, liquor, antique stores and haberdashery.

It was the day before my scheduled meeting with the local pet society that while walking along downtown Chadsworth, I heard a woman scream. The vision of her anguished face flashed into my mind and the image of a young boy dressed in faded blue jeans and a long-sleeved black shirt running at full speed in the direction Nilla and I were headed. Gripped tightly in his hand was a purse that did not belong to him; his eyes bore a mixture of confidence in his escape intertwined with fear of capture. He was quickly approaching—now only several feet behind us. In no time, he would turn the bend just ahead and be long gone bearing the ill-gotten fruits of his labor.

One could imagine how many times he'd done the same thing and gotten away with it, only to plan his next move – to stealthily lie in wait for his unsuspecting victim. I heard the squish-squashing of his tennis shoes closely behind. It was the precise moment he was about to zoom past us that I abruptly held out my cane to the left, tripping him, and watched as he fell forward, rolling over like a car tire, then ultimately landing flat on his back on the hard pavement. I dropped the leash and yelled, "Get him, Nilla!"

Nilla took off at full speed and pounced on top of the already injured boy, biting him on every spot she could manage – determined to teach him a lesson he'd never forget. He screamed and tried to push her off of him, but a man dashed over and pinned him to the ground. I made my way over to Nilla and managed to get her away from the chaotic scene. Her job was done. As tiny as she was, she made her Momma proud.

The frantic woman got her purse back and the boy was restrained until police arrived.

2

The room was almost packed to capacity when I arrived at the podium with the gracious assistance of a young man. As he went to take his seat in the front row, I proceeded with my introduction: "My name's Lucille Pfiffer—Mrs., that is—even though my husband Donnie has been dead and gone for the past four and a half years now. We had no children, other than our little Shih Tzu, Vanilla; 'Nilla' for short." I smiled, reflectively. "By the way, I must tell you she doesn't respond to 'Nill' or 'Nillie'; it's 'Nilla' if you stand a chance getting her attention. She totally ignores you sometimes even when you call her by her legal name '*Va (vuh)*...nilla'.

"We reside in a quiet part of town known as Harriet's Cove. A little neighborhood with homes and properties of all sizes. We're mostly middle class folk, pretending to be upper class. The ones with large homes, much bigger than my split level, are the ones you hardly see strolling around the neighborhood, and they certainly don't let their kids play with yours if you've got any. Those kids are the 'sheltered' ones—they stay indoors mainly, other than when it's time to hop in the family car and go wherever for whatever."

I heard the rattle inside someone's throat.

"Uh, Mrs. Pfiffer..." A gentleman at the back of the room stood up. "I don't mean to be rude or anything, but you mentioned the neighbors' kids as if you can see these things you described going on in your neighborhood. I mean, how you said some don't play with others and they only come out when they're about to leave the house. But how do you know any of this? Or should we assume, it's by hearsay?"

I admired his audacity to interrupt an old lady while she's offering a requested and well-meaning introduction to herself. After all, I was a newbie to the Pichton Pet Society and their reputation for having some 'snobby' members preceded them.

"Thank you very much, sir, for the questions you raised," I answered. "Yes, you are to assume that I know some of this—just some—via hearsay. The rest I know from living in my neck of the woods for the past thirty-five years. I haven't always been blind, you know." I liked how they put you front and center on the little platform to give your introductory speech. That way, no eyes could miss you and you think, for one delusionary moment, that you're the cream of the crop. Made a woman my age feel really special. After all, at sixty-eight, three months and four days, and a little *over-the-hill*, I highly doubted there were going to be any young studs falling head over heels in love with me and showering me with their attention.

"Pardon me, ma'am." He gave a brief nod and sat back down again.

I took that as an apology. I could see the look on Merlene's face as she sat in the fourth row from the front. She thought I'd blown my cover for a minute there, but she keeps forgetting that I'm no amateur at protecting my interests. Sure, I sometimes talk a bit too much and gotta put my foot in my mouth afterwards, but my decades of existence gives me an excuse.

I could hear Merlene scolding me now:

"Lucille, I've told you time and time again, you must be careful of what you say! No one's gonna understand how an actual blind

woman can see the way you do. They won't believe you even if you told them!"

Her words were like a scorched record playing in my brain. She got on my nerves with all her warnings, but I was surely glad I was able to drag her down there to the meeting with me that day.

I tried not to face that guy's direction anymore, even though the dark sunglasses I wore served its purpose of concealing my *blind stare.* "Thank you, sir," I said. "Well, I guess there's not much left to say about me, except that I used to have a career as a private banker for about twenty years. After that, I retired to spend more time with Donnie, who'd just retired from the Military a year earlier. We spent the next twenty-one years together until he passed away from heart trouble."

Someone else stood up—this time a lady around my age. "If you don't mind my asking…at what point did you lose your eyesight? And how are you possibly able to care for your pet Vanilla?"

When I revisit that part of my life, I tend to get a tad emotional. "It was a little over eight years ago that I developed a rare disease known as Simbalio Flonilia. I know, it sounds like a deadly virus or something, but it's a progressive and rather aggressive deterioration of the retina. They don't know what causes it, but within a year of my diagnosis, I was totally blind. I'm thankful for Donnie because after it happened, he kept me sane. Needless to say, I wasn't handling being blind so well after having been able to see all of my life. Donnie was truly a life-saver and so was Nilla. She's so smart—she gets me everything I need and she's very protective, despite her little size. I've cared for Nilla ever since she was two months old and I pretty much know where everything is regarding her. Taking care of her is the easy part. Her taking care of me is another story."

Though somewhat hazy, I could see the smiles on many of their faces. The talk of Nilla obviously softened some of their rugged features.

Mrs. Claire Fairweather, the chairperson, came and stood right next to me.

"Lucille, we are happy to welcome you as the newest member of our organization!" She spoke, eagerly. "You have obviously been a productive member of Chadsworth for many years and more importantly, you are a loving mom to your precious little dog, Vanilla. People, let's give her a warm round of applause!"

A gentleman came and helped me to my chair. The fragrance he was wearing reminded me of how much Donnie loved his cologne. Such a fine man, he was. If it were up to him, I wouldn't have worked a day of my married life.

It would've been enough for him to see me every day at home just looking pretty and smiling. His engineering job paid well enough, but I loved my career and since it wasn't a stressful one, I didn't feel the need to quit to just sit home and do nothing.

"Thank you, dear," I told the nice, young man.

"My pleasure, Mrs. Pfiffer."

Merlene leaned in as Claire proceeded with the meeting. "I told you—you talk too blasted much!" She whispered. "If you keep up this nonsense, they're gonna take your prized disability checks away from you."

"It'll happen over my dead body, Merlene," I calmly replied.

"Mrs. Pfiffer, I must say it's truly an honor that you've decided to join us here at the

Pichton Pet Society," Claire said at the podium. "With your experience as a professional, I'm sure you'll have lots of ideas on how we can raise funds for the continued care of senior pets, stray dogs and abused animals. Your contribution to this group would be greatly appreciated."

After the meeting, she'd caught Merlene and me at the door, as we were about to head for Merlene's Toyota.

"I'm so glad you joined us, Mrs. Pfiffer. My secretary will be in touch with you about our next meeting."

"Thank you, Mrs. Fairweather. I'm honored that you accepted me. After all, animals are most precious. Anything that supports their best interest, I'm fired up for."

"Did you always love animals?" she asked.

I gulped. "Well, if I may be straight with you… I hated them— especially dogs!"

Her hand flew to her chest and a scowl crept over her face. I must have startled her by the revelation.

"It was after Nilla came into our life that I soon found a deep love and appreciation for animals—especially dogs. To me, they're just like precious little children who depend on us adults to take care of them and to show them love, as I quickly learned that they have the biggest heart for their owners."

Fairweather seemed relieved and a wide smile stretched across her face. "Oh, that's so good to know! I was afraid there for a moment that we'd made a terrible mistake by accepting you into our organization!" She laughed it off.

I did a pretend laugh back at her. I may be blind, but I'm not stupid—that woman actually just insulted me to my face!

"I don't know why you want to be a part of that crummy group with those snooty, snobbish, high society creeps anyway!" Merlene remarked after we both got in the car.

I rested my cane beside me. "Because I've been a part of crummy groups for most of my adult life. I don't know anything different."

Merlene gave me a reprimanding look. "It's not funny, Lucille. You dragged me out here to sit with people who, I admit love animals, but they seem to hate humans! I've heard some things about that Fairweather woman that'll make your eyes roll. You know she's a professor at the state college, right?"

"Uh huh."

"Well, I heard she treats the kids who register for her class really badly. She fails most of them every single term. The only ones who pass are the ones who kiss up to her."

"If there's a high failure rate in her class, why would the state keep her on then?" I asked.

"Politics. She got there through politics and is pretty much untouchable. I heard she also was a tyrant to her step-kids. Pretty much ran them all out of the house and practically drove the second fool who married her insane. He actually ended up in the loony bin and when he died, she took everything—not giving his kids a drink of water they can say they'd inherited."

"I blame the husband for that."

"Not when she got him to sign over everything to her in his will when he wasn't in his right mind. The whole thing was contested, but because she was politically connected, she came out on top. After that, she moved on to husband number three. If I knew that woman was the chairperson of this meeting you dragged me out to, I would've waited in the car for you instead of sitting in the same room with her."

We were almost home when Merlene finally stopped talking about Fairweather. You'd think the woman didn't have a life of her own, considering the length of time she focused on this one individual she obviously couldn't stand. I just wanted to get the hell out of that hot car (the two front windows of which couldn't roll down), and get home to my Nilla. She'd be waiting near the door for me for sure.

I wish I was allowed to bring her to the meeting. They claimed they're all about animals, but not one was in that room. I guess I was being unfair since they mentioned that particular Monday meeting was the only one they couldn't bring their pets to. That was the meeting where new members were introduced and important plans for fundraisers were often discussed.

"I'll see you later, Lucille. Going home to do some laundry," Merlene said after pulling up onto my driveway. "Need help getting out?"

"I'm good," I replied.

"How sharp is it now?"

"I can see the outline of your face. Nothing else at the moment. Everything was almost crystal clear in the meeting."

"Yeah. Inopportune time for it to have been crystal clear," Merlene mumbled.

She was used to my *inner vision*, as we call it, going in and out like that. I grabbed hold of my cane and the tip of it hit the ground as I turned to get out of the vehicle. "I can manage just fine. I'm sure it'll come back when it feels like. Thanks for coming out with me."

I smiled as I thought of how much she often sacrificed for me. Ten years my junior, Merlene was a good friend. We had a row almost every day, but we loved one another. She and I were like the typical married couple.

"By the way, I forgot to mention, my tenant Theodore, told me this morning that someone had called about renting the last vacant room."

"Perfect!" Merlene said.

"Said he was coming by this afternoon. What time is it?"

"It's a quarter of five."

I had an idea. "Merlene, he's supposed to show up at five o'clock. You wanna hang around for a few minutes to see what my prospects are? Maybe he's tall, dark and handsome and I may stand a chance."

"I doubt it," she squawked. "Besides, I must get at least a load of laundry done today. If not, I'll likely have to double up tomorrow for as quick as that boy goes through clothes! I tell ya, ever since he met that Delilah, he's changed so much."

"Why don't you leave that boy alone?" I barked. "He's twenty-seven-years-old, for Heaven's sake! Allow him to date whomever the hell he feels like. He's gotta live and learn, you know, and buck his head when need be. You and I went through it and so must he. You surely didn't allow your folks to tell you who you ought to date and who you shouldn't, did you? And furthermore, why do you keep calling Juliet, *Delilah*?"

"Because she's just like that Delilah woman in the Bible; can't be trusted!" Merlene spoke her mind. "And since you asked—why do you call her *Juliet*? Her name's Sabrina."

I sighed. "You know why I call her that."

"I tell ya...she's no Juliet!"

"Anyway, you're gonna wait with me a few minutes while I interview this newcomer or not?" I'd just had enough of Merlene's bickering for one day.

I heard her roll up the two remaining car windows and pull her key out of the ignition. It was one among a ring of keys.

Nilla was right at the front door when I let myself in. I leaned down and scooped up my little princess. She licked my face and I could feel the soft vibration of her wagging tail. Merlene walked in behind me.

"Nilla pilla!" she said, as she plonked down on the sofa. "Why can't you assist Mommy here with her interview? After all, you've gotta live with the newbie too."

I heard Theodore's footsteps descending the staircase. His was a totally different vibration from Anthony's. Anthony's steps were softer like that of a woman's feet. I had a good look at him a few times and he definitely was *Mister*

168

Debonair. And that desk job he had at the computer company suited him just fine. Theodore was different; he was more hardcore, a blue collar worker at the welding plant, pee sprinkling the toilet seat kinda guy. That was my biggest problem with him – he wasn't all that tidy, especially in the bathroom. But I hadn't kicked him out already because he's got good manners and sort of treats me like I'm his mother. Anthony mostly stays to himself and that's fine with me too.

After I'd sat down, Nilla wiggled constantly to get out of my arms. She didn't like "hands" as much as she preferred dashing all over the place, particularly when her energy level was high. I could tell that was the case at the moment, so I gently let her down on the tiled floor and immediately saw her sprinting through the wide hallway which led into the kitchen, then doubling back into the living room seconds later, and making her way under the sofa. Under there was her favorite spot in the entire house. Often, she stayed in her hut-like habitat for hours at a time.

"Good evening, ladies," Theodore said as he entered the living room. How did the meeting go?"

"It was horrible!" Merlene replied.

"It went fine, Theodore. Beautiful atmosphere; beautiful people," I said.

"She got her fifteen minutes of fame," Merlene snapped. "That's all she cares about. She should've invited *you* to waste a full two hours there instead of me."

Theodore laughed. "Well, I'll be heading out to work. See you later."

"Yeah, later," Merlene replied.

As Theodore opened the door, he met someone standing on the other side. "Oh, I'm sorry. Almost bumped into you," he said.

Theodore went his way and the person stepped inside.

"What're you doing here, David?" Merlene asked.

"I'm here to see Miss Lucille. I'm interested in renting the room."

I could sense Merlene's shock. After all, why would her son who lives with her come to rent a room from me?

Visit Tanya's website: tanya-r-taylor.com

* LUCILLE PFIFFER MYSTERY SERIES
Blind Sight
Blind Escape
Blind Justice
Blind Fury
Blind Flames
Blind Risk
Blind Vacation
Blind Christmas

INFESTATION: A Small Town Nightmare (The Complete Series)

* THE REAL ILLUSIONS SERIES
Real Illusions: The Awakening
Real Illusions II: REBIRTH
Real Illusions III: BONE OF MY BONE
Real Illusions IV: WAR ZONE

* CORNELIUS SAGA SERIES
Cornelius (Book 1 in the Cornelius saga. *Each*

Myers Series Book 1)
One Dead Politician (Nick Myers Series Book 2)

Haunted Cruise: The Shakedown
The Haunting of MERCI HOSPITAL
10 Minutes before Sleeping

Made in the USA
Coppell, TX
21 February 2022

73858019R00098